DESTINY

BY OKON IBANGA UDOH

DORRANCE
PUBLISHING CO
EST. 1920
PITTSBURGH, PENNSYLVANIA 15238

The contents of this work, including, but not limited to, the accuracy of events, people, and places depicted; opinions expressed; permission to use previously published materials included; and any advice given or actions advocated are solely the responsibility of the author, who assumes all liability for said work and indemnifies the publisher against any claims stemming from publication of the work.

Dorrance Publishing Co
585 Alpha Drive
Pittsburgh, PA 15238
Visit our website at www.dorrancebookstore.com

ISBN: 978-1-6386-7152-7
eISBN: 978-1-6386-7685-0

DESTINY

Table of Contents

ACKNOWLEDGEMENT

Thanks to my wife and my children. The publication of this book was made possible by their encouragement and assistance.

INTRODUCTION

This book was born out of the Nigerian Civil War, which took place from July 1967 to January 1970. It is not about the war itself, as Chapter One appears to portray. However, when I thought of writing the book, my first inclination was to write about the civil war, which operation and conduct I knew a great deal about. And this was the time the civil war was a topical issue.

I saw that there were too many books on the subject and that one more addition would simply add to the diversity and multiplicity of opinions and leave the reader not wiser. Instead, I decided to look at the life of Benjamin Bassey Owen and how the war affected him.

DESTINY is the story of a brave young man who by chance got involved in the civil war and who in the same token also accidentally got disengaged before the end of the war. It is about this young man who had a vision of what he wanted his life to be. He had the plan and the determination to see it through.

The civil war interrupted his plan. But what would have ordinarily slowed him down and change the course of his life, turned out to be an instrument of acceleration toward his goal. As they say, what was meant to be a stumbling block became a stepping stone.

Without the outbreak of the civil war, Benjamin was convinced that he would have gone through his university education as the first step in pursuit of the profession he loved. He had the vision, he had the plan, he had the ability, and he had the resources. Everything was in his favor.

Benjamin did not throw up his hands in despair when the military conflict started during the summer vacation of 1967. He decided to flow with the current and join the rebel army to help to defend what he absolutely believed in, at the time. Afterall, back in the University, he was among the teeming number of students who advocated the break away of the region from the Nigerian federation.

He gave his best for the period he served as an officer in the rebel army until an event he did not anticipate took place. Again, Benjamin did not struggle against the situation that in the first place offered him no option. He went with the current. It was not very long when something—another life-changing event—happened to him that made him start to believe that there was an invisible hand that guided his affairs.

Benjamin Owen found himself being propelled to a new threshold. He saw it as another opportunity and grabbed it with both hands. His success was phenominal inspite of the many hitches and punches he received. The hardest punch came when he lost his wife and two children in a natural disaster in Oklahoma. Yet he charted a new course that eventually led him to his ultimate goal.

DESTINY does not attempt to prove the controversial concept of predestination. Rather, it tries to illustrate that "where there is a will, there is a way." Benjamin Owen was not predestined to be what he was or to go through all he went through. He beat all the odds, seized every opportunity, turned every obstacle into an opportunity, and achieved what he had willed for himself. His life was a blessing to many people both in his adopted county and also back in his country of birth. This is what he has always wanted to be. He made it his destiny.

CHAPTER ONE
THE CIVIL WAR

Lieutenant Benjamin Bassey Owen was an infantry officer at the headquarters of the 52nd Brigade of the Biafran Army at Isiokpo, Rivers State. He was undergoing a military intelligence course when he got posted to a riverine location at the outskirt of Port Harcourt to take command of a platoon of soldiers and defend the area against the invading federal troops. Lieutenant Owen joined the fighting six months after the war had started. He was not a professional soldier. He was, like the many students in the University of Nigeria, Nsukka, who championed the rebellion and were recruited and hurriedly trained to join the fast-depleting officer cadre in the rebel army.

He had spent about four weeks at the new location before the situation escalated. His troops had been prepared and deployed to defend the coastal village against the menacing federal troops. Their duty was to repel any attack by the federal troops and protect the civilian population. In the face of an attack, which was eminent, the soldiers were accordingly deployed. The civilian population in the village was equally briefed on what to do in case of an attack.

Meanwhile, the sound of artillery gunfire from the federal troops some kilometers away could be heard in the surrounding areas. The bombardment has been on intermittently for many days. For the soldiers, it was time to be on optimum alert. The villagers were in constant fear; few of them were known to have sneaked out of the village under the cover of darkness.

For Lieutenant Owen, it was a very difficult time. He was committed to the cause he was fighting, but the army he was serving was ill-equipped for the task. Personnel welfare seemed not to be part of the ethics. He was expected to improvise for his soldiers in everything from uniform to food and fight the enemy. Their food depended on the generosity of the villagers. And they were generous, perhaps more out of fear than kindness.

The bombardment became intense for a few days, then, stopped suddenly. For some days, there was an uneasy quietness. Lieutenant Owen thought he needed more intelligence on the situation. Getting the correct intelligence about the enemy is an important and indispensable factor in warfare. It can win a battle and save lives if properly used. The officer was using a few trusted villagers as his informants. They spied on the enemy troops and reported back to him. But recently, he started receiving conflicting reports from them. In fact, one of them deserted his family, left the village, and started working with the enemy troops. Lieutenant Owen no longer trusted the source and the information he received. The need to have an additional information became very crucial. The night of May 23 was the quietest night in weeks; there was no single artillery fire in 24 hours; no troops movement was reported. Such dramatic change in the situation could mean a lot of things in a battlefield. That situation made it compelling for him to take some action. Lieutenant Owen and his second-in-command, Second Lieutenant Chucks, met to consider the situation. They reasoned that the federal troops were seasoned and experienced soldiers and well-equipped; they had lost just a few battles since the war started over one year earlier. Withdrawal from the location or desertion was not an option. A frontal attack with a strong and an overwhelming army was suicidal. They knew they could not win the battle considering the formidable odds against them but did not want to be sitting ducks. They settled on ambush and a hit-and-run battle strategy. Effective ambushes could, however, delay the progress of an approaching army and dislocate its plan and allow help to come. They decided that somebody had to go on an immediate reconnaissance to get a little more information. Lieutenant Owen decided to do it himself. He planned to brief the troops that evening when he came back. That was not to be.

Although it was still drizzling, Lieutenant Owen and his aide, Corporal Nathan, set out very early in the morning. Both were armed, each with an Ak47 automatic rifle in case there was the need to use weapons. The officer wore a rain coat over his uniform. They started out walking closely to the side of the road always ready to take cover by the bushes whenever there was any suspicious approach. By arrangement, the officer always led the way while the aide followed some distance behind.

Reconnaissance in a war zone needs extra care; movement must be calculated and silently so that it does not alert anybody close by. The environment has to be carefully surveyed before making the next move. The two moved slowly taking all precautions to conceal their presence. At certain times, they had to wait and listen to sounds and movements. Lieutenant Owen was happy he was making some headway into the enemy territory without detection. He was inching close to where he believed was their headquarters; he could hear voices indicating the location of their outer defenses, which ideally should not be more than two kilometers from the headquarters. For a while, he sat down to analyze what he had learned and make some notes and thought he had gotten enough to work on.

They had been out on the job for more than two and a half hours, and it was time to go back. Like a bolt from the blue, a green military land rover came into sight as Lieutenant Owen rounded a corner on the road. There was no mistake which vehicle it was: federal soldiers he had to meet in an unpredictable circumstance. He was about 20 meters away, and the occupants of the vehicle had seen him. He was still rooted by the side of the road behind some bushes when the vehicle skidded to a stop.

Lieutenant Owen had to decide what to do in a split second: to run, to fight, or to surrender. By this time, the vehicle came to a complete stop, and five soldiers jumped out in unison as if it was a military drill. Owen had no chance to run without being shot at; he could not fight because it was impossible for him to take on five armed soldiers. He stood where he was, smiling sheepishly at the men. He was surrounded and disarmed. The soldiers discovered that the man they just "captured" was an officer, a very valuable asset.

A captured officer was a highly prized prisoner. It could earn each of the soldiers a promotion and other benefits and enhance the battalion commander's position. Owen was motioned into the vehicle and driven away. The soldiers aborted their mission and returned to the battalion headquarters with their prized prisoner. Owen reckoned the distance was about two kilometers.

What happened to Corporal Nathan, Owen's aide, was a matter of conjecture, as they never met again or heard anything of each other. Nathan, it was believed, had seen the approaching military vehicle from a safer and more comfortable distance and might have watched the little but deadly drama before his boss climbed into the land rover. He was in no position to help. He had no option other than to go back and report what he saw to the second-in-command, who would naturally and immediately take over the command of the platoon and report the incident to the Brigade Headquarters.

The disappearance of a military officer in the frontline was a very serious matter, especially in a civil war, where atrocities were common and actions often interpreted in many ways. It could be that he was captured and taken prisoner-of-war, but in this case, there was no fighting. It could be seen as a deliberate scheme by a soldier to cross to the enemy territory and surrender in order to stop fighting. In this case, that was not true and could not have been possible without a pre-arrangement. The situation in the Biafran Army might have been bad enough for the front fighters but not sufficient reason for an officer to deliberately surrender to the federal troops. It could mean a summary execution, as was the case in many unfortunate situations. It could mean indescribable torture. Nobody wanted to willingly face any of these. What happened to Lieutenant Owen might have been seen as a misadventure and letting down his guard where and when it was most needed. Nevertheless, it raised some eyebrow.

The news hit the small community hard, and tongues began to wag. Some said that he had been killed when he refused to surrender while others contended that he was taken prisoner while fighting with the federal troops; yet others thought he ran away from Biafra to join the federal troops because the Biafran military authorities were planning to get rid of him for protecting the villagers whom the authorities believed were supporting the enemies. None of them knew what actually happened. The truth is that the villagers loved Lieutenant Owen and missed him. He was their chief protector. He sympathized with their situation because the community was never trusted by the Biafran authorities that regarded them as agents of the federal government and saboteurs (a new vocabulary that became popularized during the civil war).

Lieutenant Owen knew the truth. He regularly spoke to the people in private and advised them not to provoke the authorities by showing hatred of the presence of the troops there. He encouraged them to support the soldiers with food and other things they needed and as much as possible avoid having conflict with any soldier. It was an instant death during the war to be labeled a saboteur, and soldiers could take the law into their hands. Owen succeeded during his stay to prevent any arbitrary arrest or "accidental" killing of any member of the community. They regarded the officer as one of their own, and his death or disappearance was a personal blow to many of them.

Iwofe is a small fishing and farming community about 15 kilometers northwest of Port Harcourt town. It situates on the coastline of a river by that name from where one can travel to other outer islands like Tombia and Buguma and towns like Isiokpo, where the 52nd Army Brigade Headquarters of the Biafra Army was located at the time. It was to this town that many inhabitants of Bakana were forcefully moved for "security" reasons and located during the war. Many of them who survived the constant "combing" exercises stayed there until the time both Iwofe and Bakana were liberated by the federal troops.

There was nothing special in posting Lieutenant Owen to this location. The posting was random, and it became a blessing to the inhabitants of this small community. Owen was a disciplined, committed, and compassionate officer. He was opposed to the policy of taking life as punishment for unfounded allegation, as was often the case during the civil war. To him, the only circumstance that warranted taking life was in battle. He had personally prevented the killing of people who were maliciously labeled as enemy of the cause. He once stopped the civil exercise of "combing," which required members of the community to search for saboteurs in the bushes surrounding the village. The intended result of such "combing" exercise was to eliminate people suspected of not supporting the war effort.

His troops knew how much Lieutenant Owen did to protect the people and get their support. Many of them did not like how he curbed their excesses but had to obey him as the commander of the unit. For a while, Owen did not think of what fate awaited him as a prisoner-of-war in a civil war where each commander made his own rules, or followed no rules at all. His mind flashed back to what might happen in the location that just lost him.

He wondered what conspiracy theory would be formulated about his disappearance from the scene. It was a regular feature in the military to start stories that were knowingly false and let them circulate to make the enemy look bad, weak, inhuman, and unwelcome in the eyes of the citizens.

Owen never forgot that day in May 1968. The day that betrayed his hope. The day he left the people under his care and could not return to take care of them. The day that made him miss the battle he was preparing for. Owen was a loyal and committed officer; he was committed to the cause and vowed to defend it. And for him to have been forced into the unknown, uncharted, and unpredictable future was the worst he could have asked for even in the midst of the unpredictability of the war.

Chapter Two
PRISONER OF WAR

The soldiers abandoned their mission and returned to the battalion headquarters with Lietenant Owen. It was a short distance from the scene of arrest. Owen was led to the battalion commander by two soldiers.

"He is an officer," the first soldier announced after a salute.

"We captured him on the road as he was trying to run into the bush," the second soldier added.

The captain dismissed them without any question. One could see disappointment on the faces of the soldiers who had expected some compliments and perhaps a question or two which would have made them feel they have done something great. The commander simply turned to Owen without saying a word. Owen was prompted to speak for the first time.

"Good morning, Captain," he saluted.

"Good morning, who are you?" the commander asked in not a very friendly tone.

"I am Lieutenant Owen," replied Owen.

"You are not a Lieutenant here," the commander thundered back. "You are a prisoner. You can sit down there." He pointed to a chair.

Lientenant Owen smiled and took the chair. He had mentally gone through the likely scenario that could play out on meeting a superior officer. He had expected some hostility. So far, he considered this a good beginning. Superior officers have the tendency to always want to intimidate others. Owen understood it and had planned to control the situation as much as possible. He decided not to feel sorry for himself. He would not be defiant because that could be unproductive and dangerous. He would not beg for pardon from the officer who was in no position to grant it. He had resolved to feel as respectable as he could in the circumstance. Sitting alone there for a while was very helpful for him to pull himself together and prepare for an inevitable questioning session that was coming.

Lt. Owen had heard about Captain Buhari, the battalion commander, from the series of information he received from his informants. He was described as an independent and easy-going officer who was in no hurry to prosecute the war. One of the informants who penetrated his headquarters described him as a very stern-looking man who seemed to have no interest in his work and that he had a very limited contact with his troops. He preferred to assign most of the duties to his second-in-command, a lieutenant. According to the informant, he rarely got to his office before noon, and he smoked a lot and drank heavily.

Captain Buhari was a field commissioned officer, like many officers in the federal army. He was in his mid-thirties, a very experienced soldier who rose from the ranks. At the beginning of the war, there was a shortage of officers for field command duties. To fill the gap, many of the soldiers with long experience and command capabilities were commissioned. Captain Buhari benefited from this policy. This was not his first command duty as a commissioned officer.

Lieutenant Owen was aware of all this information about Captain Buhari before he met him. He was not quite sure how this information would be useful to him now that he was meeting the officer in person. Owen knew immediately he arrived at that headquarters that he would never have the opportunity of going back to his troops. The chance of an escape was nil. Sitting there alone, Owen went through likely possibilities of what could happen to him.

As he was still pondering, Captain Buhari returned to the room. He came with his second-in-command, Lieutenant Bong. As they entered the room, Lieutenant Owen stood up in a military fashion, which seemed to have taken the two officers by surprise. The commander motioned him to sit down. Coffee was brought in a tray with three cups. Owen was served coffee and cigarettes. Although Owen was not a smoker and coffee was not his beverage of choice, he accepted both with thanks and happiness. He was not happy because he had wanted to smoke and drink but happy because smoking and drinking together was more than a symbolic friendly acceptance of an enemy officer and a potential prisoner-of-war.

The two officers started talking on issues not related to the war or the fighting or about Owen's presence in their headquarters. They talked about rumors circulating in town, social issues, and the latest local news. Owen was drawn into the discussion, and he seized the opportunity to express himself but was careful not to show how much he knew about the issues they were discussing. He was still not sure this was genuine. Owen thought it was their method of making him relax before giving them as much information as they wanted. Owen was wrong. That was not the case.

The three men had been talking for more than 30 minutes. Owen started to ponder which direction they were going. When a second cup of coffee was served, it was already past 1:00 in the afternoon, and Owen remembered that he had not eaten since morning and was feeling hungry. Owen could not have the audacity to ask for food, no matter how friendly he thought they were. As he was contemplating that they could offer him food, Captain Buhari suddenly stood up and announced that he was taking Owen to the brigade headquarters to see the Brigade Commander. Owen stood up and followed the Captain into a waiting military truck. They were on their way to the brigade headquarters. No one spoke to the other during the entire trip, which was about 35 minutes. Two-thirds of the way was through inhospitable bush track.

Lieutenant Owen had an idea of the part of city where the brigade headquarters was but was not sure of the exact location. He had a map of the city and its suburbs in his former location showing possible locations of the federal troops and their headquarters. This was a map developed by the Intelligence Unit based on the information collected over time. It changed from time to time according to the movement of soldiers. The brigade headquarters had remained in its location for more than four months, which was an indication of little progress in the fighting by the brigade.

They arrived at the headquarters at 2:20 PM. The brigade commander was standing outside his office when Captain Buhari and Owen alighted from the vehicle. The first message Owen received was shocking: There was a soldier who was brought from somewhere else to the commander. He immediately ordered the soldier to be shot. Within minutes, Owen heard two-gun shots, and the soldier was sent to his untimely death. If it was meant to instill fear in Owen, the summary execution of the soldier did not move him.

Inside the commander's office, Captain Buhari, bellowed, "Good afternoon, sir," as he saluted.

"Good afternoon, Captain," replied the brigade commander.

"Sir," Captain Buhari continued. "I am bringing a prisoner of war captured this morning in my location. He is an officer in the rebel army."

"Thank you, Captain," replied the commander. "Take him to the Intelligence Office, I will see him later."

"Yes, sir," Captain Buhari replied and saluted as he turned and led Owen out of the office.

Owen said nothing all along since he did not have to say anything. For the period, he was standing there, Owen deliberately focused on the commander, trying to study him and make an impression. Lieutenant Owen knew that he was the man he had to deal with later and that his decision would affect his life and future.

The Intelligence Office was in the same compound, two blocks away from the commander's office. The compound was an office complex with many individual buildings owned by Shell Oil Company. Captain Buhari dutifully delivered Owen to the head of the Intelligence Unit and left, having accomplished his own task. As Captain Buhari was leaving, Owen turned to him and said, "Thank you, Captain. You've been very kind. I hope that you and I will meet again."

Captain Buhari was taken by surprise. All he could say was, "God bless you." He looked at Lieutenant Amos and walked out of the building

The head of the Intelligence Unit was a man in his late twenties whom Owen later knew as Lieutenant Amos. Lieutenant Amos did not wear his uniform and rank at the time of that first meeting. In the military tradition, Intelligence officers do not wear their uniform and rank most of the time. Lieutenant Amos was very conservative and hostile and rude in dealing with people. He made himself not easily approachable.

Most of the work in the office was done by his subordinate officers. Owen was sent to the next subordinate officer, who called two younger officers to take Owen to the interrogation room. There were four young men in his office, two of them about Owen's age, one of them much older and one much younger than all of them. They were all very friendly with Owen. Owen could perceive some sign of respect for him even though he was a prisoner under interrogation. Owen was high-spirited, friendly, and extremely cooperative. Cooperation made their assignment much easier.

Owen had resolved to be friendly and cooperate, whatever the odds. He needed some friends among his enemies and determined to make the best of any contact he established. He knew that the initial report on him could determine the direction of future decision and action. He could not toy with his fate, which was, as it were, in the hands of these young men. He was confident that their hostile boss would not be able to easily discredit their initial positive report on him. To achieve his objective, Owen decided to play down on his education, one of the things the federal troops, who were less educated, held against the biafran fighters and officers.

Owen was academically better educated than any of the people he had met so far. Professionally, there were certain things they did that Owen knew were not right. He would not tell them that he had been in the university before deciding to enlist in the army when the war broke out. He would cover those years with other activities without any of them being able to know; besides, they would not afford the luxury of looking for anybody or source to corroborate his story. He would keep to himself how much he knew but would not lie about what he did not know to impress them. Owen was familiar with the routine in the interrogation of enemy combatants or suspects. He had done it himself.

In the interrogation room, the two young soldiers went through the usual stereotyped questions coming straight from a standard interrogation manual:

"What is your name?"

"How old are you?"

"Where were you born?"

"Where did you go to school?"

"When did you enlist in the military?"

"What is your rank?"

...And a lot more questions, some seemingly irrelevant but asked to discover if the person interrogated had told the truth. Other questions included how many troops he had in his location, what kind of weapons the soldiers use, where he had been in the last six months. The objective of an interrogation is to obtain information, any information that could be of use to the military seeking the information.

Owen had no difficulty in answering all the questions. There was really nothing important to be revealed about the Biafran Army that was not known by the federal military authorities. Owen was a field officer and knew little about the running of the headquarters and told them as much as he knew. He avoided telling them what he did not know, considering the fact that they had other sources of information. The most important thing was to be convincing, and Owen was convincing. He demonstrated the readiness to let them know all he knew about the army they were fighting against. He could sense the feeling of satisfaction in the two interrogators. The interrogation would continue the following day.

Owen was relieved when he was asked to spend the night in the intelligence building. He was shown a little room, big enough to take a bed less than one meter wide and what could pass for a mattress. The toilet, which was shared by many others, was a few meters away from the room. Before then, Owen never gave any thought to where he was going to spend the night. He did not even remember that he had not eaten all day. Now that he was a guest of the Intelligence Unit for the night, he started to think of what would happen to him after the Intelligence officers finished with him. He tried to ward off the thought of his immediate future because he was not yet in a position to determine it, but it kept on coming back. As he squatted on the bed and was struggling with his thoughts, the door opened and somebody entered with a plate of food and a cup of water.

That was his dinner. And it happened to have been the only meal he had that day. It was a plate of boiled rice in palm oil with a little piece of beef meat on top. It was without any taste, and there seemed to have been more sand than rice in what was supposed to be rice. Ordinarily, Owen would not touch that kind of thing called food. But he was hungry and was not in a position to choose what to eat. Owen gobbled it down and drank the water that came with it. However, he was thankful that somebody remembered that he should eat.

He was also thankful that he had a bed to sleep on, whatever the description. He never expected anything to be normal again in whatever happened to him since the incidence of the morning of that day. His little worry were the mosquitoes he had to contend with that night but he believed that the lack of sleep in the past 36 hours and the excruciating events of the day would make him sleep without feeling the bites of the mosquitoes. Owen had enough time to pray, and he prayed for a long time before falling asleep. The ordinary day in his life ended in an extraordinary way in a strange military location.

O   O   O

Owen woke up with a start just before dawn after seven hours of sleep. For a very long time, he had not slept that long, yet he was still feeling tired. He cleaned up and made himself ready for the day's ordeal. The morning was quiet, as most of the personnel of the headquarters were still not out to their duty posts. Those who were on sentry duty during the night were still there waiting for dawn to come for them to be relieved.

Owen did not want to be seen loitering round, so he kept very close to his room whenever he was not inside. It was very uncomfortable to stay inside the small windowless compartment. Besides, he was still in the trouser and T-shirt he came with the previous day, which incidentally constituted his sole wardrobe. He did not know the time, but he guessed it would be another three hours before the soldiers arrived to begin where they stopped the previous day, and before then, he had to endure the inhospitable condition.

It appeared to him that he was the only guest of the Intelligence Office. Nobody else, he observed, visited the toilet. He could not hear any sound of footsteps on the narrow corridor; no noise whatever. Owen thought that his stay there for the night might have been a special privilege as an officer who still had some questions to answer. He felt greatly relieved when one of the soldiers from the

Intelligence room went to invite him to their office, certainly, for further interrogation.

Before the interrogation started, Owen had decided to make the morning exciting and friendly. He exchanged hearty greetings with them and asked them each about their welfare and their families. He was surprised about the amount of discussion he evoked among them, talking as if they had known him for years. It took a little time before they settled down for business.

The interrogation was a follow up to what was done the previous day, a mop up, as it were. Nothing new really came up. They needed some explanations to some of the things Owen said. He happily and willingly explained all they wanted to know. One thing Owen wanted to avoid was volunteering information. He answered all the questions, gave them all they wanted, but did not volunteer any information. Even at those times Owen spoke with them on other general issues, he was careful about what he said because some careless slips could bring unpalatable consequences, not minding the smiling faces and friendly attitude of the Intelligence officers.

By 11:00 that day, the interrogation was over, but Owen still remained a guest of the Intelligence Office. He believed that the report could go to the brigade commander the afternoon of the same day. He could not imagine what was going to happen to him, so he sat down there trying not to worry about it. He spent all day in the office dozing. At the end of the day, Owen was taken to a house occupied by two officers in the same large compound and asked to stay there with them.

Owen had neither choice nor a say in whatever happened to him at this stage. He was constantly praying that the worst would not come. The officers he was asked to stay with were both field commissioned second lieutenants – Second Lieutenant Duba and Second Lieutenant Ola. Lieutenant Duba was an infantry officer while Lieutenant Ola was from the Signal regiment. They were both in their mid-twenties and part of the brigade headquarters personnel. The house they stayed in had two bedrooms and a shared living room. The only place Owen had to stay was in the living room, where people were moving in and out. He spent the first night on a sofa in the same dress he wore since he arrived the previous day. How he managed himself was his business; his only privilege was to eat from the common kitchen where the soldiers took their food.

Owen spent the following day in the house lying on the sofa most of the time, expecting that he could be called anytime. Night came, and he spent his second night on the sofa with people entering and leaving the room. He was summoned to appear before the brigade commander on the third day. He was literally taken at gun point into his office. The office was large and furnished with chairs lined along three walls with the commander's big empty table in the middle of the room.

Owen stood in the room facing the commander like a prisoner awaiting sentencing from a presiding judge. The soldier who took him in made sure that Owen stood far enough to avoid 'contaminating' their commander.

"Good morning, sir," Owen remembered saying involuntarily. The commander ignored the greeting. Instead, he shouted at Owen.

"Tell me all that you know about the rebel army."

Owen honestly did not know how to answer the question. He knew that the commander had seen the report from the Intelligence office on his desk. Still looking straight at him, Owen said gently and slowly, "Sir, I have already told you all I know," referring to the report before him.

The commander flew into a rage and ordered that Owen should be taken away and shot. Owen's answer was regarded as an affront and an unwillingness to show remorse. Owen did not show any emotions; he said nothing. His feelings were more of confidence than defiance. As two soldiers rushed into the room to take Owen away, he looked at the commander straight into his eyes before he was pulled away. He did not beg for his life as perhaps was expected.

The commander was momentarily unsettled about the lack of show of emotion by Owen, even when he was taken away to be shot. Moments later, he shouted again and ordered the soldiers who were still within a hearing to bring back Owen. Inside his office, he ordered that Owen should be returned to where he was staying. Ordinarily, one could not make sense out of what appeared to be an irrational behavior of the commander, but as a strong believer in the direction of human affairs by the higher cosmic powers, Owen was not disturbed.

As Owen stepped out of the office, he noticed some soldiers and civilians gathered in the vicinity of the office.

It appeared that they had had a pre-knowledge of Owen's appearance before the commander. Meanwhile, the news of a captured Biafran Army officer had spread in the camp. The few people who saw him described him as a handsome looking young man. Those who did not see him were anxious to see him because they thought he could be killed. There were still many Biafran sympathizers especially among the civilians' commandeered work force, who privately prayed that Owen should not go the way many others had gone.

After that incidence, Owen learned that the commander was Lieutenant Colonel Edie James. The name indicated that he was from the same geographic and ethnic area as Owen. The details Owen knew later revealed that Colonel James' hometown was a mere 10 kilometers away from Owen's village. The commander was little known in his home because he spent most of his time in Lagos and other parts of the country where he served in different military establishments. Ethnic affiliation could be a strong factor in taking a decision such that the commander faced. Owen believed it could be but, having gotten a glimpse in the thinking of military men, never assumed anything. Indeed, what happened next was enough to confirm his position and shake the ethnic belief.

The brigade commander, Colonel James, was 29 years of age and about five feet, six inches tall (1.7 m). He was not a man of great personality. He made up for what he did not have with a domineering character and pomposity. He was both feared and respected in the camp by both officers and soldiers. Many of them preferred to stay out of his way unless sent for. Only his personal defense corps and those in charge of his domestic needs could be seen around him.

His strict code of discipline kept every soldier under his command always at alert. He worked hard and showed commitment to the cause. The divisional command had little supervision over his operational activities because he had proved himself as a dependable brigade commander. He took over a brigade of soldiers who were noted for running away from the frontline and transformed them into fighting men. His men faced most of the tough battles in the southeast zone of the war theater.

Beneath his toughness, however, was a warm and sociable character when it was time to relax. There were many social events created at the headquarters from time to time. The commander would always be seen as cheering and dancing with the troops. At such times, officers and men were treated as friends and not as soldiers. That was a little peep into the life of the man who would decide the fate of Lieutenant Benjamin Bassey Owen.

O   O   O

Owen had been at the brigade headquarter for days since his arrival. Nothing substantial had happened except one threat to his life. Nobody has spoken to him since then, and the hope of being sent to a prisoner-of-war camp was dwindling. The officers he lived with were friendly; they had lively chats most of the evenings when they came back to the house. Owen avoided a situation where any talk would center round him. He felt making them know too much about him was not in his interest.

What happened with Benjamin Owen was a little odd. He was kept sitting in the living room of two junior officers at the brigade headquarters apart from the one day he was threatened a summary execution. The commander did not need consultations to decide what to do with a "captured" enemy officer delivered to his headquarters. The rules of war are there to follow, although they were often ignored. But indecision was not an alternative.

As Owen was wasting away from the indecision, the loud celebration of Biafra's "independence" provided an opportunity for the commander to be reminded of Owen's presence in his headquarter.

CHAPTER THREE

OWEN SPENT TIME IN GUARD ROOM

May 30 was a landmark in Biafra. It was on that day that the Eastern region of Nigeria unilaterally declared itself independent as Republic of Biafra, seceding from the Federal Republic of Nigeria. The act of secession was the immediate cause of the civil war. The rest of the country decided to go to war, crush the rebellion, and return to the status quo while the rebellious region, now Biafra, took up arms to defend its "sovereignty." Owen was fighting on the side of the secessionist regime before he was captured and taken prisoner.

The war was bitter and unpredictable. It divided families and friends. People who were living and working together as Nigerians found themselves as enemies fighting in opposing armies. Many did it as their patriotic duty; for many, the circumstance of the situation forced them to fight in self-defense. Whatever reason there was, each side believed that it was fighting a just war. The political leadership on both sides made the points and urged the rest of the citizens to follow.

Yet, many on both sides were reluctant followers. There were many people in Biafra, especially those outside the Igbo ethnic group, who saw themselves as being forced into a war they did not want and had no stake in. They reluctantly supported the war having found themselves physically living in the territory called Biafra. Many escaped being killed in the north and had to flee to the eastern region. For them, Biafra was home and had to be defended. Many championed it out of emotion, and there were those, especially those in the corridor power, who needed the war for political and economic reason. The last group was thinking of events in a Biafra after the war.

When hostilities started in July 1967, each side promised a quick and decisive action to defeat the other. After one year of fierce fighting, Biafra was still strong to commemorate its independence.

Biafra was celebrating the anniversary of its independence on this thirtieth of May. Despite the ongoing hostilities, the Biafran leadership rolled out drums in celebration. The leader of the breakaway country, Lieutenant Colonel Emeka Odumegwu Ojukwu, was known for his long passionate, inspiring, and moving speeches. He prided himself as Oxford University educated and first university graduate to enlist in the Nigerian Army.

His confidence was also based on his family wealth. His speech that day was marathon and moving. He spoke among many things, of the heroism of the Biafran people, the strength of the brave fighters of the Biafran armed forces, and the coming liberation of Biafra. Owen had no means of listening to this radio broadcast. He did not even remember the day nor its significance from the "prison camp" where he was. The brigade commander was listening to the broadcast the same way other happenings in Biafra, or what remained of it, were monitored.

Unexpectedly, Owen was summoned to see the commander. He had no idea why he was summoned. Immediately, he entered the office, and Owen realized what the problem was as he heard the broadcast of his former commander-in-chief. He was struck. Visibly angered by what he heard, the commander shouted:

"This bastard is still talking. You tell me what you did for him." Without waiting for any answer, he continued, "You fought in that rebel army. You should be supporting our effort. He is still talking and boasting." He stood up, making a gesture as if he wanted to punch Owen. "Take him away and get him shot!" he shouted at his armed bodyguard, who was standing by the door. He gave Owen no chance to say anything, not that Owen had anything to say in that circumstance.

For the first time, Owen feared for his life. He felt a chilling sensation through his nerves and a cold sweat. He wanted to speak, to say something, anything to change the momentum, but could not open his mouth. He could not understand what was happening to him. He momentarily lost his consciousness as he was pushed out of the room. He did not hear when, like in a previous case, the soldiers were ordered to return him to the room. The commander did not address Owen this time but ordered that Owen should be taken to and kept in the guard room.

The guard room is a prison house in a military camp where military personnel who commit minor offences are sent to stay as penalty for their offence. They usually serve a specific number of days, depending on the gravity of the offence. Some are also tried in addition. The most common punishment is the isolation of the soldier and deprivation of liberty. Those serving guard room punishment stay behind bars most of the time. They may also be given additional punishment in non-military duties. Corporal punishment may be meted in serious cases. Guard room punishment was designed to dehumanize the victim and take him out of circulation for a while. He is not allowed to wear the uniform during the period.

An inmate may be allotted a single cabin if his punishment was total isolation or he was violent or the guard decided to keep him alone. Otherwise, they were usually herded into one cell and locked up like animals in a pen. Where the cell was small, as many were, the inmates had to fight for space to sit down. The food was terrible, usually rationed and served in a common container where they had to struggle to take a portion. Water ceased to be a necessity. Taking bath was a luxury, and as a result, the inmates were stinking like the rooms, they stayed in. To answer to nature's call depended on the guard who has to release the inmate and escort him to the toilet. Fighting in the guard room was a constant scene, and the fact that the guilty party—or everybody involved—could earn additional time was no deterrent. Soldiers dreaded being sent to the guard room. This was the kind of place Owen was sent to, to spend unspecified period.

Generally, guard room punishment was strictly for the other ranks, not for officers. Officers were usually sent to the officers' mess if there was reason to punish and restrict movement. Owen was not in a position to make any claim of any right. He had no rights in the circumstance. He was to stay there for an unspecified time. His former commander-in-chief made a broadcast that offended the brigade commander. Owen had to be punished for that.

He was lucky in a way, the small room he was assigned could take only three inmates. Owen spoke with them occasionally but never revealed who he was. The two men were complaining bitterly how they were thrown into the guard room without committing the offences they were accused of. There was very little room for each of them. The floor was bare and cold. Inmates were not allowed to take their clothing into the guard room; they stayed in their underpants only. Owen sat on the bare floor in his bare body and leaned on the wall for support. Under that condition, it was difficult to find sleep.

The only thought that occupied his mind, no matter how hard he tried not to think of, was the Biafran leader. His speech that day earned Owen the detention in the guard room and nearly cost him his life. It might have indeed cost hundreds of innocent lives. It kept on recurring, Colonel Ojukwu, Biafran head of state, son of one of the richest men in the country, was always proud of being an Oxford University graduate, first enlisted university graduate in the Nigerian Army infantry. He always spoke "oxford" English, and his patience was short with those who did not belong to his class. He was noted for his long usually nocturnal speeches and believed that was what defined him and separated him from others. Nothing else mattered but his interests. Owen stayed late into the night with these recurring thoughts until he drifted into an uneasy sleep in his first night in the guard room.

During the next day, Owen spent most of it in the cell, which was always locked except when food was served or an inmate wanted to answer the call of nature. This was the pattern of daily life in the guard room. After two days without bath, Owen had to beg to go to the bathroom. Unfortunately, there was no water but the breathing of a little fresh air outside had a refreshing effect on him.

Owen spent four sordid days in the guard room, and they were the worst days in his life as far as he ever remembered. He was finally released and sent back to where he stayed before. It was not long before another incident occurred that caused him to be summoned before the commander for another death sentence. This was more serious than the two previous appearances.

O   O   O

Two weeks after Owen was released from the guard room, the brigade headquarters was attacked by enemy troops. Apparently, some Biafran troops had infiltrated through the front lines and found their way close to the headquarters and started an attack before dawn. The defense platoon was caught by surprise and unprepared. They suffered few casualties. By the time they fought back, the damage had already been done. The fighting ended in less than one hour, which meant that the enemies did not intend to capture the headquarters but only to harass and return.

Owen knew that the rebel forces did not have the capacity to fight a sustained battle, capture a place and keep. They depended on a hit and run tactic that could only cause damage, few casualties and a setback. It worked because the federal troops were generally caught napping. The Biafra plan was to prolong the war until it could get international assistance either to fight or to settle the issue in its favor.

After the fighting had died down and about noon, Owen was dosing in a chair from lack of sleep when a soldier entered and picked him up to go and see the commander. To Owen, this had now become a routine affair whenever something happened at the headquarters. He thought the commander wanted to swallow his pride and ask him to help. He was wrong. Owen was verbally abused, berated, and blamed for the attack and asked to explain how the rebel troops came close to the brigade headquarters. He was condemned once again and ordered to be executed. Once again, as in the previous cases, the order for execution was rescinded as fast as it was given, and Owen was allowed to live for another day. That day did not take long to come.

O O O

Owen had been in the camp for six weeks. For that period, it appeared that he was to blame for anything that did not go well in the camp or the least irritation the commander had. Owen was thinking of how to handle the situation when another attack occurred. This time, it was more serious. Owen knew that he would be sent for by the commander after the fighting, and he was prepared to tell the commander what he felt.

The attack started at night probably 3:00 AM and continued until about 8:00 AM. This attack appeared to have been well planned and coordinated from two flanks by the rebel attackers. For more than four hours, there was continuous firing on both sides and occasional night flares. Every officer and soldier from the commander himself were up and engaged. All the soldiers in the camp were ordered to join the defense platoon in the fighting. By daybreak, reinforcement came from one of the battalions, and it was then and only then that the rebel soldiers were dislodged. The injured were ferried to the field medical unit in the camp for treatment while the dead were buried in a makeshift burial ground outside the camp. Later in the day, the seriously injured were taken to the airport to be conveyed to Lagos.

Many people were afraid that the brigade headquarters could be overrun, considering the sustained fire power of the rebel troops. The consequences of that would have been catastrophic, especially for people like Owen. Although the fear sometime came over him, Owen knew from experience that the rebel fighters would eventually be forced to retreat after their ammunitions ran out. And that was what happened. By daylight, they had expended all the ammunitions they had but not before they had inflicted much damage to the federal fighting spirit.

As Owen had expected, even before all the losses were counted, he was summoned to meet the commander in the evening of the same day. Owen prayed for courage; he had decided to speak and defend himself this time. He has known the commander's usual style of intimidation and fear of being challenged. Owen would counter that this time to save his neck; it could be his last fight, but he had to fight.

Inside his office, the commander asked the soldiers to leave. He was alone with Owen. For a brief moment, Owen thought the man wanted to do the job himself when he pulled out his service revolver and placed on the table.

"Please…" Owen started, when the commander asked him to stop. Owen looked at him without betraying his fear.

"What kind of man are you?" the commander asked rhetorically. "You have been in this headquarters for five weeks, and we have encountered two attacks directed by your fellow rebels. What part have you played in these attacks?" Before Owen could say anything, he started again. "I am going to kill you myself if I find out that you play any part in it. You should be helping me but …" He did not finish the sentence when an officer came into the room—one of the two officers Owen was staying with. Owen was asked to leave the room. The two spent about 10 minutes in the room before the officer left. Owen went back into the room.

He was startled when unexpectedly the commander released a life bullet from the pistol he kept on the table. It was not aimed at Owen, but instinctively, he bent down as if he was dodging the bullet. For the first time, Owen saw the human side of the man; he smiled, and for the first time, called Owen by name then addressed him.

"Owen, so you are afraid to die? Why did you join the rebel army then? Is that why you left them, because you did not want to die? And you believe that you are safe here?" All came in quick succession, and apparently, he did not expect any answer. Owen wanted to say something, but the commander waved him away and ordered him to be returned to the house. Owen, the proverbial cat with nine lives, survived once again.

Two days after this attack, something chilling happened at the brigade headquarters. In the midst of his travails, Owen was specifically called to watch a scene of sordid cruelty. It was at about 11:00 AM; he had heard some unusual noise of people outside, but as was usual with him, Owen did not want to unnecessarily bother himself with so many things happening in the camp, so he remained inside until a soldier from the defense platoon went to invite Owen "by the order of the commander." Owen knew by experience that the commander's invitation always meant problem for him, so he was prepared for whatever the commander had in store for him. It was different this time; the invitation was for sight-seeing.

It was a chilling sight. Waiting outside the block was an open truck of people wailing and shouting. They were about 30 or 35, men between the ages of 15 and 40, with a handful of elderly women. Beyond the truck, were some young men busy digging what was undoubtedly a mass burial ground. When their work was done, the people in the truck were forced to jump into the mass grave. The "lucky" ones were shot dead first, but many others were still alive when they were buried. Their cries, pleadings, and prayers seemed to have been buried with them because nobody heard them. To the small crowd there, it was an entertainment of sorts. There were, however, some, mostly women, who broke down, hid their faces, and were sobbing.

This was more than Owen could have imagined. The shock gripped him. Why was he invited to watch the inhuman show? Was it to show what could happen to him if the commander so decided to end his life? Before he could get over the shock, another bizarre show came on the scene.

Two four-wheel drive army vehicles, each driven by an officer, moved slowly into the "killing field." Behind each vehicle was a man tied to the vehicle with a long steel chain. The men were dragged along the rough ground as the vehicles slowly moved side by side as if on a parade. First, the men's skin peeled off, then the flesh and the bones. They still cried for mercy where there was none while their strength lasted, until the vital energy returned to the Maker. The men died in a most painful, gruesome, and undignified manner Owen had ever seen or even imagined.

Many among the onlookers were gripped with fear and unvoiced hatred for the perpetrators; others were indifferent while a sadistic few enjoyed the show. It was not that Owen did not witness isolated killings and deaths from time to time since the war started, but killings of this magnitude were the most brutal, barbaric, and sadistically ingenious that he had ever witnessed.

These men and women who were killed in this most inhuman and barbaric manner were not soldiers; they were civilians who called themselves Biafrans, who refused to run away from their homes and were accused of not cooperating with the federal troops and supporting the breakaway Biafra. None of the accusations could be proven to be true.

Surely, Owen learned something, if he was invited to watch and learn a lesson from it. He started to think of how to cooperate with the commander and the personnel at his host headquarters. That was the first time the thought of planning to leave the headquarters occurred to him.

Unknown to Owen, the brigade commander had set up a surveillance ring round him after he was released from the guard room. Owen believed that the two officers he stayed with were reporting on him. They once in a while discussed and asked him questions Owen believed were to get certain information from him. The officers discovered that Owen was always staying ahead of them. They did not see anything strange with Owen; he had nothing more than a pair of trousers, a shirt, and a pair of sandals. The towel and the bed cover he used were given to him by a soldier in the camp, a relation he met when he arrived at the camp. He did not leave the house except to go to get food from the kitchen next door. He had no contact with people, and there was no way he could have been implicated in any plan to attack the headquarters.

Owen wondered how long he was going to live that way, being blamed for what he knew nothing about. He decided to help himself in any way he could. He decided to engage his hosts, Lieutenant Duba and Lieutenant Ola more in discussions, since they were the only two people he saw regularly. Talking with them, he thought, could open up a lot of things and bring more confidence among them. After weeks of close interactions, the two officers discovered how knowledgeable Owen was in both military and non-military affairs. They started to frequently consult him in many challenging issues. At a time, they urged Owen to enlist in the Nigerian Army. Owen, on the other hand, suggested to them that he could work with the military as a civilian.

Owen knew that the war was not going to end soon, and the most challenging thing to him was how to leave the war zone and not to sit there waiting for the war to end. Enlistment in the army was not the answer to his problem. He could do that and get stuck as a soldier and not an officer. The brigades had the power to enlist local people as soldiers but had no authority to enlist officers. Owen, in any case, had no inclination to enlist even as an officer. His ambition was to find a way out of the situation before circumstances forced him to do what he did not choose to do.

Soon the conversation with the two officers veered toward Owen's idle time and wastage of his talents. Owen did not discourage them from discussing him this time. He knew that one of them, being an infantry officer in-charge of the defense platoon, met with the commander frequently and was likely to discuss him with the latter sometime. Owen was right. Most of the things they discussed always filtered to the commander. It was not long after they discussed the work of the field Medical Unit and the shortage of personnel when Owen got another surprise.

Lieutenant Duba was excited when he came into the house that afternoon. He told Owen that the commander

Owen was right.

had asked if Owen could go to work in the brigade field Medical Unit. The Medical Unit was used for emergency treatment of wounded soldiers before being transferred to the hospital. It also functioned as a clinic for sick soldiers; it dealt with all medical problems in the brigade. Seriously wounded soldiers were evacuated to Lagos for further treatment.

By this time, Port Harcourt Airport had opened for military flights only. Later, the Red Cross and other humanitarian planes were allowed to bring in relief supplies and also help in evacuating wounded soldiers. The Medical Unit of the brigade was in charge of taking the wounded soldiers to the airport and loading them on the planes. Working in that unit afforded the personnel there to have regular access to few people outside the military units. Owen thought working in the Medical Unit would give him the opportunity to go out to the airport once in a while, more importantly relieve his idle and monotonous life in the camp and offer him the opportunity to talk to other people.

It was the officer in charge of the Medical Unit, Captain Martins, who invited Owen to his office the very next day, apparently at the instruction of the commander. Captain Martins was not, strictly speaking, a soldier. He was a paramedic who joined the medical corps to perform medical duties only. He was given a short service commission based on his professional experience and level of relevant education. His interview with Owen was short. Then he briefed Owen extensively about the work of the various sections of the unit. Owen was not assigned to any particular section; he performed all duties wherever he was assigned. It did not take long for Captain Martins to acknowledge Owen's ability, ingenuity, and commitment in handling issues in the clinic.

After three weeks of performing general duties, Captain Martins asked Owen to move to the section, which was in charge of evacuation of badly wounded soldiers to the airport. This section was also in charge of preparing dead soldiers for burial. Owen was excited to be sent to this section but would not show it. He was not sure if the soldiers knew who he was and how much they would trust him. Captain Martins knew him, and Owen had made special effort to impress and win his trust and confidence.

His first day to the airport was the first time he ever left the camp since he arrived there four months earlier. On that day, he, with five soldiers in the section, took 20 wounded soldiers in five vehicles to the airport. The airport was not far away from the brigade headquarters; even with the bad roads and security check points, it took 40 minutes to get there. They arrived shortly before the military plane landed and had enough time to complete the documentation.

It took some time to load the soldiers on the plane. Those on wheel chairs were wheeled in, those on stretchers were carried in, and those who could stand were supported into the plane. It was a pretty tough job, but the soldiers handled it very well. They had to wait until the plane departed before they returned to headquarters. Going to the airport was a daily business; on most days, they made two trips in mid-morning and late afternoon.

At other times, when the fighting was heavy and there were more casualties to be evacuated, they did make more trips, all during the day because there were no night flights as a matter of military security policy.

Meanwhile, Owen was making more friends with the people around him. One of such friends was a talkative young man whose stock in trade was gossiping. He kept Owen informed of all the happenings in the camp, from rumors of summary executions to who has got a new "wife" from the war front. From the information gleaned, Owen learned how lucky he was to still be alive. He was happy that he was no longer directly under the commander's radar and his frequent emotional and killer outburst to the detriment of Owen.

Owen devoted his entire time to his work; of course, there was nothing else to get his attention. He was also thinking how he could free himself finally without waiting for the war to end. He knew that it was not safe for him to try to leave the camp in such a militarized environment. His thoughts were focused on how he could get on one of those flights run by the humanitarian service to Lagos, where he would take a chance.

There were two humanitarian bodies that came into Port Harcourt airport from time to time with relief supplies and sometimes took wounded soldiers back to Lagos or abroad. They were Medicins Sans Frontieres (Doctors without Borders) and Caritas, a Roman Catholic relief agency, and the soldiers in the Medical Unit had access to them when soldiers had to be evacuated. After serious thoughts, Owen decided that he would take a chance with one of these airlines. He started observing if there were some friendly crew members he could rely upon when he took a move. He waited patiently. It was not very long when he had the opportunity to take the first step.

Medicins Sans Frontieres flight seemed to have been a better choice for Owen. He had been going in and out of the plane each time it came and took wounded soldiers, and after doing this for a long time, Owen decided it was time to do something. There was a young woman who was a regular crew on this flight; she was friendly and approachable and had tried to speak to Owen once or twice before. Each time, Owen had cautiously avoided speaking to her in the presence of the soldiers. Owen was biding his time and did not want to try anything that would fail. However, he felt convinced she could be of use to him in his plans. He decided to test the waters in her next visit. It was not long when the chance came.

The plane came again in four days. Owen was the first person to approach it when it landed. Once inside, he saw the woman and went straight to her. In a surprise move, the woman stretched her hand to Owen and said, "I am Anne."

Owen, not expecting that action, heard himself saying, "I am Benjamin," as he shook her hand, using his first name for the first time in many months. Before Owen could say something else, he saw other members of the medical team coming in with their patients. He quickly turned away and left the plane to go and bring another patient. Anne was no doubt surprised by his action, but as a veteran of the humanitarian body, she understood it. She had been on that job for a long time and had experienced actions like that prompted by circumstances of the person.

Other members of the team did not see the short encounter with Anne, and Owen made sure they never saw it. Owen believed, and rightly so, that he was still under surveillance, and his contact with Anne, if reported, could cost him the privilege of going to the airport. The only witness to the cordial exchange was a wounded soldier, who had other things to worry about than a friendly exchange between a visiting crew member and a military employee. Owen was happy the way the first contact ended; he believed that it would make the woman think that Owen was not in a secure position to speak freely with her. The next opportunity, Owen reasoned, would play out better to his advantage.

That next opportunity came in two weeks. The flight landed about 11:00 in the morning. Owen and his team arrived 15 minutes after with 30 wounded soldiers. They had little time left and so started working in earnest. Each time Owen went in with his patient, he made a brief eye contact with Anne but never said anything. The plane had been on the ground longer than was expected, and the loading was not completed. Owen still had one patient to load; he deliberately allowed others to finish so that he would be the last. He wheeled in his patient, positioned him, and moved inside the plane instead of coming out. He met Anne and without any ado whispered to her, "I want to come to Lagos."

Anne had witnessed many such situations in the course of her work where people desperately wanted to leave their country and war zones. She directed Owen to a half-concealed seat in the corner of the plane without saying a word. The baggage hold had closed, and Anne was doing the final checking. For the first time in a very long time, Owen's heartbeat started to race. He was not quite sure if it was true that he was finally leaving the war and the unfortunate situation behind him. He did not consider the consequences of his action if the plan failed or what will be done to the soldiers with whom he worked; he was consumed by the fact that he wanted to leave the war zone. It did not occur to him that he had no plans of what to do in Lagos; all he wanted was to leave the war zone and free himself.

Owen had always lived a life of commitment and loyalty to his duty. The work he did for the military was no exception. But in this case, he was torn between duty and his safety and future. He chose to take a risk for his future. He had thought out the situation and the circumstances, that as long as he had a trusting guide and a reliable friend to take him out of the front-line battle zone, all other things would fall in place. He certainly knew that if he could get into Lagos, tracing him would be impossible unless he ran out of luck. Again, he reasoned that he was anonymous, and the brigade commander would not report his missing since they would have a lot to explain.

Anne, as Owen sized her, was very knowledgeable in the affairs of the war and compassionate in dealing with people. She knew the turf, and Owen had imagined where her sympathy would be. Her English was perfect except if you were bilingual in French and English, you would not have any inkling she was French.

The last barbaric show in killing those civilians, and the fact that he was specially invited to see, sent chilling thoughts each time he remembered it. Now that he was out of the camp, if something went wrong in Lagos, and he was arrested, he would not be returned to Port Harcourt. In Lagos, he would have a chance that he was not likely to have in Port Harcourt.

CHAPTER FOUR
ESCAPE TO LAGOS

His heart was still pounding when the plane taxied for a takeoff. Twenty minutes into the flight, Anne went to Owen; they discussed for some time. The first thing was to get him safely into Lagos and get him a place to stay before thinking of what next to do. Owen just realized that he had to depend completely on Anne for some time. He had no plans nor was he able to think of anything he would do in Logos.

Anne Dupont was 30 years old, a French national from Lyon and a social worker. She had worked with Medicins Sans Frontieres for 10 years and in four different war zones round the world. She had dealt with refugees, with people who tried to flee war torn areas, and with people who had faced all sorts of calamities. She knew the contacts to make to seek help for the needy, and she had succeeded over the years in settling few of them in other foreign countries. Her first contact with Owen indicated to her that the latter might need help. That made it easier for her to accommodate Owen when he finally approached her. She assumed that Owen had nobody to take care of his affairs in Lagos and decided that she would do more than taking him into Lagos.

The plane landed in Lagos in 55 minutes without any incidence. Owen could see many military ambulance vehicles already lined up waiting on the tarmac to evacuate the wounded soldiers to the hospital. A little fear gripped Owen; was it possible that the brigade headquarters in Port Harcourt could inform the military authorities at the airport to arrest and detain him? Owen argued that it was not possible. It would take the soldiers 40 to 45 minutes to get back; there was no means of communicating with headquarters before then. Taking into account the chain of command in the military, by the time the commander would be informed that he was missing, Owen would be clearly out of the airport area; after all, Anne had promised to see him safely into Lagos.

Owen knew that it would be difficult if not impossible for the brigade to officially pursue him. To start with, his presence at the army brigade headquarters in Port Harcourt for those four months was ambiguous to say the least. He was not officially declared a prisoner-of-war nor was he treated as such; the only resemblance of that was his interrogation by the Intelligence Office, which could apply to any suspect. Owen's presence in the brigade was never reported to the higher military authorities, which ought to be the case. For the brigade to report Owen as missing or escaping from military custody, would expose the brigade's ineptitude and worse still, endangering the fighting forces by keeping an enemy officer without adequate security and reporting his capture to the army headquarters. Owen concluded that there was no danger from the command he had just escaped from. It had no locus standi to legally pursue Owen.

After the wounded soldiers were all taken off the plane and driven out of the airport, Anne went back and escorted Owen out of the plane and out of the airport. She hired a taxi that took them into town. She said nothing to Owen during the taxi ride, and Owen was wise enough not to say anything to her or ask her any questions. Traffic on the route was heavy, and it took one hour to get to the destination.

Meanwhile, there were commotions at the brigade headquarters in Port Harcourt. At the airport, Owen's teammates did not suspect anything until it dawned on them that the plane had taken off with Owen inside. It was not something any of them could explain whether it was an accident or a deliberate act. They knew that they would have to answer for the lapse. The most senior of the soldiers would assume the responsibility and explain how Owen had gone to Lagos with the plane, and they were unable to detect and stop it.

A written report had to be submitted to the commander through the head of the Medical Unit. Captain Martins questioned the soldiers but would not indict any of them. He submitted the report to the commander the same evening and recommended that the soldiers be punished for lacking in vigilance. He took an interim step to remove all of them from the section handling evacuation of wounded soldiers. They were deployed to other sections.

Evacuation of wounded soldiers to the airport was seen by soldiers as both duty and privilege. It allowed the soldiers to leave the camp almost every day, which was what soldiers cherished much. The soldiers used the opportunity to make contacts and send personal messages through to Lagos. The loss of this privilege was not considered a punishment; they would be punished appropriately when the report got to the commander. So, they waited.

The news of Owen's escape spread like a wildfire in the camp. Owen had suddenly become a very important figure and a symbol of stubbornness and challenge to the commander. The blame for his flight was not put on anybody yet.

The commander invited Captain Martins for discussion after reading the report. He knew that he could not report the incident to the army headquarters and ask for help to arrest Owen. In the first place, the presence of Owen as a "prisoner-of-war" was illegal; it was not reported to the army hierarchy, and to report his disappearance would bring unpredictable consequences which nobody wanted to contemplate. Besides, his flight to Lagos could not be considered to constitute any danger to the course of the war. The only official existence of Owen was in the files of the Intelligence Office, which could be removed so that Owen ceased to exist. The brigade commander, whether he was advised or not, did not take any action on the report. The soldiers were not punished either, and the case died a natural death. Owen did not exist as far as the Nigerian Army 16th Brigade was concerned.

Anne stopped the taxi some distance to the hotel, paid off the driver, and walked the rest of the way to the hotel with Owen. It was a small, two-star hotel lying some distance from the main road. Owen was checked in as Mr. Douglas, and he never questioned it. Owen sat on the edge of the bed while Anne sat on the only chair in the room facing each other for the first time since they first met in the plane. Owen thanked Anne profusely for her assistance; the latter said nothing. It was getting dark outside. Anne stood up, told Owen that his dinner would be brought to the room, that she would see him the following morning then handed Owen some money and left.

Owen had a good dinner, no doubt the best in many months, took his bath and then discovered that he had nothing to change into. That was the least problem for him; after all, he had stayed for months before in one dress. He lay down and involuntarily went through the events of the day but prevented himself from thinking about what would happen the next day. He fell into a deep sleep, and for the first time in many months, he slept without fear.

When Owen woke up, the sun was already up and shining brightly into his room. He remembered that Anne was coming that morning, so he had to prepare to meet her. He could not go to the restaurant and was reluctant to use the telephone to make an order. He was dosing off again when he heard a soft knock on the door. As he opened the door, Anne was standing there beaming with laughter. As if it was contagious, Owen found himself laughing too but quickly checked himself.

Once in the room, Anne handed Owen a bag; in it were some clothes, a pair of shoes and sandals, and other things Owen would need. She sat down and went straight into business. She began to address Owen.

"Mr. Benjamin, tell me your story and what you want."

"Thank you, Anne," Owen started, "I have never met such a kind and understanding person like you before in my life. My name is Benjamin Bassey Owen." Owen went through where he had been and what he had been doing since the time he enlisted in the Biafran Army, how he fell into the hands of the federal troops, his stay in the brigade headquarters, until the time he met Anne at the airport. Anne listened attentively without any interruption and at the end asked him few questions and wanted to know about his life before he enlisted in the military.

Owen had little choice; he told Anne his entire life history from his birth in a small village Biase in eastern Nigeria in 1948, his early education in the local school, to the time he was in the University of Nigeria, Nsukka, and up to the time he joined the military to fight on the side of Biafra. Anne took him to task on many points which appeared to her inconsistent. Owen learned quickly the kind of person he was dealing with; Anne was precise in her thoughts and language and incisive in her decisions.

She felt satisfied in the discussion and the information she extracted from Owen. Having brought Owen to Lagos, she decided not to abandon him, but she wanted him to decide what he wanted. Owen's desire was to go back to the University and complete his studies but was unable to say how he could be helped in that; besides that meant he would have to remain in Lagos for almost one year before he could get an admission into any Nigerian University.

After talking for about two hours, Anne realized that Owen was in no position to make any realizable decision for himself at that moment. Although Anne felt that she should not carry the burden of deciding for somebody she has just rescued, the circumstance dictated otherwise. She had the experience and contacts Owen did not have, she could move round and get things done, so she realized that she had a duty to guide and see him through. She took a decision, but Owen would not be privy to it yet. Before she left, she gave Owen some more money and advised him that he could go out if he so wished and promised to see him in four days.

Anne started making contacts for Owen to be granted a refugee status in France. In her position in Medicins Sans Frontieres, she knew she could handle that. The four days she promised Owen were not enough to conclude any arrangements, but she still decided to see Owen that evening. The visit was brief. She told Owen that she was working on a plan to send him to France under the United Nations refugee laws. She explained that in France, with the right contacts, Owen could start his studies and begin a new life.

Owen knew that France was not the easiest place for him to go; he did not speak French, and unlike in places like the United States and Great Britain, he knew nobody in France. For Anne, it was easier to get him to France than any other place; she had the contacts and associates who would help Owen in France. That was the decision, and Owen had no choice in it but to accept. He was, however, happy about it. Meanwhile, he would remain in Lagos for arrangements to be completed. How long this would take, Anne herself did not know. Before she left that evening, Anne gave Owen two manuals of the French language to help him start learning the language. It would take some time before Anne would be able to see Owen again.

○ ○ ○

Owen had been in Lagos for 35 days and was still in the small hotel room. He started feeling the boredom of inactivity. Anne had encouraged him to go out since, in her view, there was no perceived danger. He was doing very well in his French and hoped to both surprise and impress Anne in her next visit.

Owen had to be granted a refugee status before a visa could be issued to him to enter France. Medicins Sans Frontieres had applied on his behalf and was awaiting the outcome. Anne was sure it would not be rejected since Owen was officially in its custody. Bureaucracy, however, had to take its course.

Owen had no close relations in Lagos; those who were there had returned shortly before the war started, but he was sure there were still a few of his townspeople there who had refused to leave Lagos. He was sometimes tempted to look for them, but his sense of personal security was stronger than the sense of relationship. He resolved to remain incognito until he was able to leave Lagos and find himself a new life in France.

Meanwhile, the news that Owen was either taken to Lagos or he escaped to Lagos had reached his village, which was a mere 200 kilometers from Port Harcourt. His family and indeed the whole village knew he was still alive. Owen was a rising star in his community and the envy of many of his peers.

He was the only one selected out of 10 candidates who went for enlistment in the army officer corps from the village. At that time, the military was considered as the only viable industry in spite of the danger involved in the fighting. All schools were closed; nobody was employing anymore; everything in the society was geared toward the war effort. Apart from the idleness, many young men wanted to join the military to avoid the constant harassment by the men in uniform. Owen was seen and considered a very lucky and inspiring young man. He was in the university already, and he enlisted in the military as an officer and was travelling away from home again. Soldiers did not make matters easy for young men who were still walking the streets. Soldiers had become the new elite group in the "country."

It was a relief to many people in the village that Owen was still alive. Six months later when the news reached the village again that Owen was in France, he became an enigma. His peers in the village could not believe the fortune of this man. They were unaware of the pains Owen went through.

Meanwhile, Owen, still in Lagos, had reconciled himself to the situation. He did not know what had happened to his parents and siblings. He was the third of seven children in the family. He tried not to worry about the situation he neither knew nor could control. His entire focus was on being able to get some help and move on. So far, he believed that the help he needed was within his reach, and his thoughts were on how he would take advantage of the expected generosity of the French government and people.

After 16 days of no contact, Anne turned up at the hotel. It was a happy meeting. Owen had been granted a visa into France, a ticket had been purchased for him, and Owen knew when he was to leave Lagos for Paris. Anne delivered the things Owen would need on his trip in a suitcase. She spent the rest of the time briefing Owen on his trip, what he should expect and needed to do on arrival in France. She also briefed Owen on the cultural peculiarities of the French.

It was an opportunity for Owen to surprise Anne on how much French he had learned. He also told Anne of his successful trip to the University of Lagos. Anne bid Owen goodbye and departed, feeling very happy that Owen was added to the list of her accomplishments in her humanitarian work.

Owen's flight was scheduled to depart Lagos international airport, Ikeja at 6:00 PM on November 16, 1968. It was 3:00PM when the 18-seater bus pulled up at the front of the hotel, and Owen, who had been waiting at the lobby, stood up ,expecting to see Anne. She was not there. Owen went into the bus where there were 14 other passengers already; he scanned the bus before sitting behind the driver. Anne was not there. Maybe she was at the airport, Owen thought. There was nobody he could ask. It turned out that 12 of the people in the bus were going to France as refugees. Only two were women.

The airport was a short distance, and there was little traffic at that time of the day. It took the driver 30 minutes to be there. When the passengers alighted, Owen observed that each of them carried one new suitcase similar in size, but not color, to the one he carried.

Owen looked round; still there was no Anne. He pretended that he was not disturbed but decided against asking the two officials who were with them. He convinced himself that it was not Anne's duty to be at the airport. After all, she had bidden him goodbye at their last meeting in the hotel.

The officials directed them to a separate counter for checking in, just behind where others were checked. The check in was thorough and detailed. They had to answer questions about their background, where they lived, why they sought refugee status in France, etc., etc. At a point, Owen thought he could be turned back, and Anne was not there to defend his application. Eventually, all was fine, and all of them were directed to the departure lounge. The two officials from Medicins Sans Frontieres were still there with them until it was time for boarding.

It was a smooth five-hour flight to France. The Air France took them to Charles de Gaulle airport in Paris. For all the 12 refugee-seeking passengers in the plane, it was their first time to fly that long and also the first time to travel outside Nigeria. Even though all of them knew that they were travelling under the same circumstances, there was no discussion among them in the plane. They simply behaved like fish out of water. One could see that they were full of excitement for leaving the country at such a terrible time and also fear of the unknown.

CHAPTER FIVE
A REFUGEE IN FRANCE

The plane arrived in time in the early hours of the morning on November 17, 1968. Winter did not set in fully, but as would be expected, it was terribly cold for Owen and others who had never experienced winter conditions in their life. The officials who waited to receive them had expected that, so they brought some clothing to keep each of them warm.

They went through the immigration formalities on a separate counter. The two officers who manned the counter were very friendly and made a lasting first impression on them, as Owen later recalled. They were directed into a bus and driven straight to a compound at the outskirt of Paris, a place that was to be their temporary home for the coming months, or perhaps years for some. Since it was still dark by the time they arrived, they were directed into their rooms to spend the rest of the morning hours in bed until they would be met formally and instructed on the new life they were going into.

Each person was shown into his room. Owen occupied a room with three other inmates, men about his own age.

The room was scantily furnished and looked very much like a shared college dorm with no privacy. Each occupant had a small compartment for personal things. There were two baths and two toilets attached to one end of the room.

The temporary settlement camp, as it was called, comprised of one- and two-story buildings, out as far as the eye could see. It was a large complex constructed to be an independent community. The living quarters had buildings for families to live together and different structures to house single people. It could take a maximum of 400 people. At the time Owen arrived there, the population of the camp was about 250 men, women, and children from different countries and nationalities. It functioned like a typical social and economic community in which members were engaged in various normal everyday activities.

Apart from the living quarters, there were many other buildings in the camp for various functions. There were instruction and briefing rooms, there were rooms for recreation including games, television viewing, and reading. There was a library, a cinema theater, and a gymnasium. There were various workshops located at strategic places for those who were interested in learning trades. The camp also had a school for children as well as for adults. The soccer field close to the school provided the opportunity for young adults to practice and play soccer and also train in athletics. There were few shops located at strategic points to offer items of daily needs at subsidized prices. The camp provided sufficient facilities to cater for the immediate economic and social needs of the refugees.

Feeding in the camp was communal for many inhabitants. They ate from the same kitchen, and the food was prepared by volunteers among them. Families that opted to prepare their own food, were given appropriate quantity of food according to the size of the family. That choice was, however, not available to single people. The refugees who had spent some time in the camp and had jobs in the city were not compelled to eat in the camp if they did not want to. The rules were flexible in many aspects of life in the camp to help the refugees to adapt fast to their new life.

The documentation of the new arrivals who came in that morning did not start until about 12:00 noon; they were allowed to catch a few hours of sleep. For some in the party, including Owen, sleep was a far cry; they lay awake all through the hours. They did not anticipate the degree of cold they experienced in their new place of abode, and they knew they had to adapt to it.

During the documentation, they got to know one another; they all claimed to come from Biafra, but the officials at the camp advised them to put Nigeria as the country of origin. Each of the 10 men and two women had a different story to tell why each was granted a refugee status in France. France was in fact a strong supporter of the short-lived Biafra and offered enormous assistance, including the acceptance of many people from the war-ravaged area as refugees.

After lunch, they were assembled again in one of the briefing rooms for a comprehensive briefing. Briefing took the whole afternoon and part of the following day. Subjects of briefing included: France in the world; the French and its culture; social and political norms; and understanding the French language. Other issues were the instructions and regulations governing their stay in France and in the camp in particular, and the initial conditions for movements outside the camp. Emphasis was placed on the necessity to obey the rules of the camp. They were officially designated as refugees having fled from the war in their country and were being accepted for a temporary stay in a different country and accorded the refugee status as defined by the United Nations statutes. They were ready to start a new life of regulated living, which was, after all, not as bad as it sounded.

Refugee camps, by definition, were not to provide permanent living conditions. Refugees had the freedom to return to their home countries as soon as the conditions which forced them to leave their countries in the first place ceased and life became normal. While they stayed as refugees, it was the responsibility of the host country to help them live a life as normal as possible.

The camp authority tried to make the refugees live a normal life. They were engaged in various meaningful activities, like cleaning up, working in the common kitchen, and doing simple maintenance work. The children attended school and the adults learned some trade of their choice. Many of them took paid jobs outside the camp, subject to the approval of the camp management. Games and sports were integral part of the camp life. There were facilities for soccer, basketball, lawn and table tennis, gymnastics, and running. The camp tried to cater for everybody's interest. Each person was paid something for the services he or she performed. A little portion of the earn-ing was given to them for their use, and the remainder saved and given to them at the time of their departure from the camp.

Owen was picked to teach in the camp school. He joined 15 other teachers; most of them spoke French in addition to their native language or English. The language of instruction depended on the language the students spoke, but all of them were encouraged to learn French, which was the major language used. Owen spoke little French, the little he started to learn before leaving Lagos. The immediate and most important objective he set for himself was to speak and write French in the shortest possible time.

Owen decided to take every advantage of the situation. The camp was insulated from the hectic life of the society. The condition was ideal for him to study. The sport facilities provided him enormous opportunities for recreation and training. He could do anything he wanted at his own pace. He made do with everything provided in the camp and the stipend he received from teaching. When he was not teaching, he spent his time in the camp library. He sometimes had to request a book not available in the camp, from a library in the city. He set himself a dateline to go back to the university, either in France or in the United States of America, for his studies. He knew that was achievable.

Owen did not see himself as a refugee. He regarded his stay in the camp as a rare opportunity and the hand of God in his affairs. He convinced himself that he lacked nothing and should not worry about anything.

The news of continued fighting at home did not dampen his optimism, after all there was nothing he could do to alter the situation. As more people arrived from Nigeria as refugees with stories of atrocities by soldiers and great suffering among the civilian population, Owen appeared not to be moved. Nevertheless, once in a while, the thought of not knowing what happened to his parents, his siblings, close friends, and former colleagues would trouble him. He kept himself busy at all times to ward off idle thoughts. His stay in the refugee camp would change his attitude to life.

It was not long before the camp authorities took notice of the kind of life Owen was leading and started to take special interest in him. In three months, Owen could speak and write perfect French. Most of the time, he would interpret to the people he came to the camp with. He was permitted to leave the camp whenever he requested because he never failed to return at the time he was required to come back. He was always called to speak to other refugees whenever there was a misunderstanding. The authorities recognized him as a leader, if one was needed.

It had been the policy of the refugee camp to issue work authorization to refugees who found suitable work outside the camp. The work had to be between 6:00 in the morning and 6:00 in the evening and must be vetted as authentic and meet the permissible category of work. Despite this liberal policy, it was difficult to qualify to work outside. The major obstacle, in many cases, was the language which was the key to integration in the French society.

Owen applied for a job in an architectural firm and got the authorization. He had no problems; he could communicate in French and had proved himself trustworthy. The firm was located only 30 minutes by bus from the camp. For him, this work would not only provide the extra income he would make but would also revive his interest in architecture, which was his major in the university he attended before the civil war forced it to close. The authorities were pleased to issue him a work permit as a reward for his exemplary work and behavior in the camp. Owen, on the other hand, promised to continue to carry on with his responsibilities in the camp, with some adjustment in timing.

The work in the firm was not difficult for him; it was within the area of his competence and interest. As was usual with him, it did not take much time before he blended well into the system. With two years of academic work in architecture, he was able to work on specialized areas without the guidance given to newcomers in the career. The firm was pleased to exploit his knowledge, as much as Owen was to refresh the knowledge he needed to continue his career. He brought in a lot of innovations that sometimes surprised his employer.

His accomplishment at work did not make him forget to pursue his other objectives. He used the opportunity outside the camp to search for his friends in the United States, where he believed he wanted to go. He soon established a contact in the New York area. One contact led to another, and before long, he was communicating with five of his friends who were in the United States. Each of them encouraged him to travel to the United States, where they said he would have more opportunities for anything he wanted.

Owen did not know how to transit from his status as a refugee in one country to the freedom of going to a third country shedding off the refugee garb. There was nowhere he could look for help; he did not want to share his thoughts and plans with anybody for fear of being upstaged. He started doing some research on his own. He read the rules of the United Nations *High Commission for Refugees* dealing with the treatment of refugees and their rights. He read about the discharge and evacuation of refugees generally and in France in particular. As Owen was trying to wade through this new problem, something unexpectedly happened.

It was on a Saturday morning, the beginning of April. The spring weather was mild and beautiful. Owen had been out for an early morning exercise in the gym and was just back to his room thinking of the day ahead when a message came that somebody was looking for him. This was the first time somebody had to look for him since he came to the camp. Owen did not know what to make of this; nevertheless, he dressed up and went to the office.

What a pleasant surprise! There she was. Anne was standing before him as he entered the room. Owen could not contain his excitement as Anne embraced him. Owen kissed her and then started speaking in quick succession.

"Comment tu vas Anne? Quand est-ce que tu arrivé à Paris?" Asked Owen. Translated as "How are you, Anne? When did you arrive in Paris? Asked Owen.

"Je vais très bien, et toi?" Anne replied. "Je suis arrivé cett matin." Translated as "I am very well, and you? Anne replied. "I arrived this morning".

Owen and Anne continued to chat excitedly, all in French. Anne was surprised to hear how much French Owen was able to learn in four months. Owen spoke flawlessly without any accent. It confirmed the genius Anne saw in Owen the first time she saw him in Port Harcourt, which made her decide to give him the material assistance he needed. She was so proud of him that she could not resist the temptation of telling the camp administrator how she met Owen. Owen was permitted to leave the camp for that day with Anne, if he so wished.

Anne and Owen went into the city. Anne wanted to show Owen round all her favorite spots in Paris. They first went to the restaurant and thereafter to the theatre to watch a play about the life of Abraham Lincoln, the famous American president. Anne had missed a lot at home for the period she spent in Nigeria, but one day stay in Paris could not make up for that, and besides, she was considering the places and things that would also interest Owen. They visited a few more places Owen had suggested. In between whatever they were doing, Anne had to brief Owen of the situation in Nigeria regarding the on-going war.

Anne was from Lyon, a city in the southeast of France on River Rhone. She intended to spend her vacation there but was in Paris primarily to see Owen, as she wanted to brief Owen of the war situation in his home and also assess his progress in France. She told Owen that from her assessment, the war would not last another year. Everybody was tired, especially the fighting forces. The civil population was weary of supporting the war. The cost in human and economic resources was getting too much to bear. Biafra had been geographically reduced to a few provinces around Umuahia, the new capital.

Owen was delighted to see Anne at that particular time when he was trying to solve a major problem. To him, Anne was Godsend. Anne was the only person Owen believed he could confide in; there was nothing he would not tell her. This was an opportunity to let her know what he was thinking of doing and to seek her advice and guidance. Owen laid his plans before Anne. After detail discussions, Anne requested a little time to think about it and make few consultations.

Anne was prepared to do anything to assist Owen. She never forgot the impression Owen gave her. As a humanitarian social worker, she had met literally hundreds of people in need at various degrees. Owen was the only one she could recall who showed such honesty and human dignity in the face of a problem that could have caused him his life. He was calculative, confident, and ingenious. Anne remembered him as one of the few men she had met who never set tears to curry sympathy and get help. She wanted to do a little more for Owen at that time; he needed somebody to trust at the time he was all alone and needed some support. Anne wanted to support Owen to realize his great potential.

Owen was away from the camp again all day the following Sunday. Among other places, Anne went with him to visit some of her friends she thought could be helpful to Owen in case he needed some more help when she left, including a professor in the City University. Anne would have recommended the City University for Owen if he wanted to study in France.

At that time, Owen had made up his mind to study in the United States and conveyed that to Anne. Their discussion thereafter was on how he would be able to leave France and travel to the United States in July. Anne knew what needed to be done to ensure that would happen. She decided to spend one more day in Paris to get things going for Owen and facilitate the process. They agreed that Owen should continue to live in the camp but use the address of the architectural firm where he worked for all his communications. Anne would speak to the refugee camp authorities to facilitate Owen's disengagement and release at the beginning of July.

The other remaining issues involved the United States embassy in Paris regarding the issue of entry visa. Anne had also made enquiry to ascertain the conditions for the issue of a visa. She had passed the information to Owen and was assured that Owen would be able to handle it when the time came. Everything regarding Owen's impending trip to the United States was tidied up by the time Anne left Paris for Lyon to spend the rest of her vacation.

It was a very happy meeting, a most satisfying three-day period. Owen was very happy he could find somebody he trusted and who trusted him too and was able to help solve his problems. Owen recalled the words of Jim Reeves that, "a stranger is a friend you do not know." Anne was a friend indeed. She made a call to Owen from

Lyon to ascertain everything went well. By mid-May, Anne called again to inform Owen that she was going back to Nigeria to continue her work.

Owen started to prepare for his trip in earnest, following the time table he and Anne had established. In the first week of May, Owen, armed with the documents from the refugee authorities, went to the Nigerian embassy located on Victor Hugo Avenue to apply for a national passport. Following the peculiar circumstance, it took one week to issue the passport.

Securing a visa into the United States by a non-European was not as easy as Owen was made to believe. But with the groundwork Anne did when she visited, Owen was able to get all the documents needed to enable him to attend the first interview. Another interview was scheduled for Owen to show proof of admission into a university in the United States and the means of financing his stay and education.

Owen was working closely with his friends in the United States. It was their responsibility to get the admission for Owen and secure all the financial and other documents the embassy would need to satisfy the conditions for the issue of a student visa. His friends kept their promise to provide the needed documents directly to the embassy. By second week in June, Owen was invited by the embassy to go and pick up his visa. That same day, Owen sent message to his friends in America and to Anne in Lagos to inform them of the success in securing an entry visa into the United States of America.

Owen was a lucky man. He also worked hard to get what he wanted. He went to France as a refugee, and he worked hard to ensure that he was going to the United States, not as a refugee but as a student. He, however, had to thank his friends in the United States who helped him to obtain the documents that qualified him for a student visa and Anne for her invaluable advice and work, which helped immensely to facilitate the process.

With barely five weeks to his departure date, Owen started the process of disengagement both from the refugee authorities and the architectural firm. His good standing with the authorities and his proven ability to pursue an independent and purposeful life stood him in a good stead to obtain the clearance and discharge from them. The only thing now on his mind was his finances. He did not, however, envision much financial difficulties.

Owen had been saving part of his meager earnings since he arrived at the camp. In his calculation, that appeared to be sufficient to get him a one-way ticket to New York. He also understood that the Refugee High Commission may assist in sending a former refugee home at the end of his stay in the camp. Apart from these, he received a normal wage paid to workers performing the same duties in his work at the architectural firm. Ninety percent of his earnings there was committed to savings. Owen was prudent when it came to spending money, and like in other things he did, he was always meticulous.

Besides all these, Anne had promised Owen some financial assistance before she went back to Lagos, but true to his nature, Owen had decided that he was not going to ask Anne for any pecuniary help. In his estimation, which was true, Anne has single-handedly done so much to give

Owen a future and a new life. His friends in the United States had assured him that he would get a scholarship and other financial assistance to continue as soon as he started his studies. Owen was upbeat that everything had gone so well with him that he had nothing to worry about. He was right.

By mid-June, Owen took the next action on his time table. He gave notice to leave his work at the architectural firm at the end of June, although he was not required to do so. Sure enough, his boss would miss the invaluable contribution he had made in the short period he had been at the firm. He understood why Owen was leaving and encouraged him in the career he has chosen. On June 28, the boss and three other colleagues took Owen out for lunch to demonstrate their appreciation, mark his last day at work, and bid him a good bye. It was one of the finest moments for Owen.

At the end of the sumptuous luncheon, there was another surprise for Owen. The boss handed him an unsealed envelop as a parting gift. Owen was stunned when he opened and saw its contents. The amount of money in it was enough to carry Owen through two academic sessions in the university. Owen never forgot the gesture.

O O O

The seven and a half months Owen spent in France was the most rewarding and fulfilled time in his last few years. France was good to him, and he sometimes felt guilty to leave the country that treated him so well, so soon. Owen was also reminded that whatever happened to him in France was a reflection of himself and his attitude toward people and society, that he got exactly what he deserved. He was a good man, an honest person, and a responsible citizen of the world. He always worked hard and left his impression on the lives of people he had contact with. Above all, he had a vision. And it was time to close this chapter of his life and begin a new one.

CHAPTER SIX

OWEN IN THE UNITED STATES

July 2 was a typically hot summer day in Paris. By 9:00 in the morning, the outside heat was almost unbearable. The parks and swimming pools were full to capacity with people who wanted to make the best out of the summer condition. The weather reminded Owen of life in the tropics where the sun never failed to show up with its tormenting heat. Owen had been up very early that morning, much earlier than usual to perform his morning responsibilities in the camp. He did all that was expected of him even though he would leave the camp for good in a few hours. Owen was a popular figure in the camp, and his departure would naturally be felt by many in the community.

A few days earlier, the news had reached many people in the camp that Owen would leave the camp for good. The other Nigerian refugees did not quite understand because they knew that the civil war was still raging fiercely at home. The camp authorities had, in their update, confirmed that they would continue to stay in the camp for some time. Many of them thought that what they heard about Owen was the usual camp rumor. Owen had actually confided in few close friends that he was in fact leaving the camp, but not for home in Nigeria. They knew that he was going to the United State to study.

Owen packed his suitcase the previous night. It was the same suitcase he brought to the camp seven and half months ago, and there was not much to pack anyway. He looked at his 28-inch suitcase and smiled; it contained all his earthly possessions. His passport, travel ticket, and other documents were neatly arranged in a leather notepad given to him by a friend and former colleague at the architectural firm.

His flight to New York's JFK airport was scheduled to depart Paris at 4:00 that afternoon. The airport was 40 minutes by train, and Owen planned to leave by 12:00 noon to give himself enough time to explore the beauty of the famed Charles De Gaulle airport before check-in time.

At 10:00 that morning, Owen went to the camp office to meet the management staff according to an earlier arrangement. The purpose of the meeting was for Owen to sign his discharge papers and be debriefed. Debriefing was part of the last rituals for departing refugees and included among other things information on the situation and life at where the former refugee was going back to and his experiences while in the camp. Owen's ceremony was particularly important to the management of the camp because he was adjudged an exemplary character and was on record to have spent the shortest period in the camp. His sojourn in the camp was all in all a happy story made out of a usually unfortunate situation.

Since the officials had known that Owen was travelling to a third country, he had to be briefed about that country. So, Owen had some briefing about the United States and the things expected of him on arrival. The ceremony, attended by officers of the camp and other refugees who wanted to, lasted for an hour.

An elated Owen said goodbye to the officials and others who attended the briefing ceremony. He looked at the camp for the last time and would remember it as a place which contributed to making him and was out of the gate in 10 minutes.

Owen arrived at the airport just before noon. He had plenty of time to look round the airport before time to check-in. He had not seen a structure like that in real life in beauty and in complexity. He enjoyed every bit of the one-man tour of the airport, and as a budding architect, he saw many things ordinary eyes did not see and learned a lot from what he saw.

The departure screen indicated that the flight would take off on time. Owen moved toward the departure area to start the formalities. After checking in his suitcase, he had no other things to carry except his notepad. The officials looked at him strangely as he went through immigration and security procedures. It was rare to find an economy class passenger without a hand luggage; Owen attracted a little attention. It was time to board and say goodbye to Paris.

The Air France Boeing took off from Charles De Gaulle Paris Airport at five minutes past 4:00 in the afternoon. From his window seat, Owen took a last view of the beautiful city of Paris that has played host to him for the past seven and a half months. He was going to America with enthusiasm and optimism to do more than just passing through it, and not as a refugee.

Most passengers were sleeping throughout the flight. Owen hardly closed his eyes for the five and a half hours the flight lasted. He was seated next to a young lady aged about 20. She was a regular traveler on the route since the age of 17. Her parents lived in France and she has been spending her summer vacations in the United States since she turned 17. She was now going to live in Massachusetts for her studies and would be visiting Paris on vacation. She spoke both English and French fluently. Owen found her talkative and useful.

After few minutes of discussion, she discovered that Owen was visiting the United States for the first time and volunteered to lecture Owen on everything about the country Owen was going to for the first time. They discussed issues, argued on ideas, and compared aspects of life in America and France. Owen learned a lot from the discussions they had and was himself surprised of how much knowledge he had accumulated. They discussed in both English and French.

The most intriguing issues the young lady emphasized, from Owen's point of view, included the freedom and independence Americans enjoy, the idea of children taking the responsibility for their lives after the age of 18, the mobility of the population, and the freedom to settle anywhere in the United States. Owen could find little comparison with his own country. Oma, as the lady was called, expressed a lot of sympathy when Owen told her what was happening in Nigeria. That prompted her to delve into the history of the Civil War in America and how the society became better after that. At 20, Oma was an encyclopedia of American history. Oma and Owen admired each other and decided they would remain friends.

Time passed quickly and before they knew it, they heard the pilot requesting everybody to fasten their seat belt as the plane was descending into JFK airport in New York. Oma invited Owen to go with her to their home in Massachusetts, but the latter politely declined. She gave Owen her contact address, and Owen promised to contact her since he had no known address to give to her. Owen contacted Oma after one week and remained in constant communication, even for the period she would spend in France.

By the time the Air France Boeing touched down at JFK airport, it was 30 minutes past 4:00 in the evening. It took 10 minutes to get into the airport building and another 30 to go through the immigration. Owen walked into the open hands of his friends who had been there for the last 45 minutes.

One of them was his former classmate who left Nigeria to return to the United States just before the war started. His father was among those Nigerians who saw the war coming and acted in time. He had been a long-time resident in the United States, who decided to leave the country for good. The timing proved to be wrong, because four months into his stay there and still trying to resettle, he started to sense the drums of war beating. He had to hurriedly return to the United States with his family. Owen became their guest in their Manhattan home. He was assured of a place to live as long as he wanted to stay. Owen was thankful for the offer, but his plans did not include living in New York.

Owen did not show any excitement of being in New York, which was rather unusual. He behaved as ordinary, as if he had lived there all his life. His main concern and priority was an immediate follow-up on his applications for admission into a university. Owen's arrival coincided with the anniversary celebration of America's independence on 4th of July. His friends had planned, among other things, to visit Washington DC, the Capital, to show Owen round and for him to watch the festivities first hand. They also planned to show him important landmarks in New York on a later date. Owen showed little or no interest in all that and had to be persuaded to visit Washington. His friends understood his concerns and sympathized with him. Owen was not a difficult man, but all he needed at this time was one thing that consumed him.

Owen availed himself of the first-hand information he got on his arrival and revisited his earlier decision on which part of the country he wanted to live and so which universities he wanted to go to. He still wanted to study architecture and to live in the south or southeast. He had chosen the state of Florida, Texas, and Georgia in that order of preference. Why he preferred these areas was not quite clear since architecture, his subject of major interest, was offered in many universities all over the United States.

Be that as it may, Owen had arrived in a free county and where the choice was limitless in many things, including where to be educated. It was just the beginning of a new life, and he wanted to live unhindered. Owing to the peculiar circumstance of his application, Owen had to travel to the universities he had applied for admission. He decided to go to Florida first, where he had applied for admission to study architecture at the University of Tallahassee. Owen was very optimistic in getting an admission in at least one of the universities of his choice, so when he left New York after five days to go to Florida, he had no plans of returning.

Owen flew from New York to Jacksonville and travelled three hours from there by road to Tallahassee. The administration offices were still open by the time he arrived, so he decided to go to the Foreign Students Admission office where he met an officer who asked him to come back the following day. He went back the following morning and started discussions with the admission officer. Owen was asked to produce the documents showing the pre-admission qualifications he claimed to have on which basis he was seeking admission. He could not produce any document because he had none with him. All he did was trying to explain the circumstance of the civil war that made him leave Nigeria without any personal documents. His argument was that he should be tested to see if he qualified to be admitted into the department of architecture.

It was difficult for Owen to convince the officers who handled this case to grant the exception this case seemed to be. At the end of the argument and consultations within the faculty, Owen was given what was termed a concession. Owen could be admitted to do a one-year prequalification course before enrolling in the department of architecture, subject to successful completion of the course. Owen was not a beggar who could accept anything; he said that much and turned down the offer. Owen left Tallahassee the following morning and headed for Texas.

After his failure to secure an admission in the University of Tallahassee, Owen started to recall the discussion with Oma six days earlier in the plane from Paris to New York. Oma, as it were, was lecturing Owen on mobility of persons and ideas, freedom to choose, and a country of opportunity. Here was an opportunity, Owen thought, he offered the university to show flexibility and do something it might not have tried before by simply testing him for admission. Owen hoped to engage Oma when he wrote to her.

In the University of Texas at Austin, Owen decided to adopt a different approach. First, he decided to go directly to the department of architecture instead of going to the Foreign Students Admission department. Secondly, he would emphasize the war situation in Nigeria and how he came to the United States, and thirdly, he would try to persuade the department to test him. He also thought that arguing in the department would give him the opportunity to speak in the language of the subject he was seeking admission to do. That might convince the lecturers to offer him a test, which he was confident, would do well. Owen insisted on going to the department of architecture when he was directed to go to the Admissions department. His theory was based on the personal appeal he hoped to make to the lecturers in the department to give him a chance to prove that he was worth the trust. That plan worked.

Owen was offered an admission into the University of Texas at Austin, School of Architecture that afternoon. It was not without a struggle. Recall that Owen went to France as a refugee; he had no opportunity to take any personal documents, or anything else for that matter, before he left Nigeria. When he went to the university at 310 Inner Campus Drive to discuss his admission, he had no documents to prove his pre-admission qualification. This was unconventional. In an attempt to prove his case, he had to disclose the circumstance that made him go to France and finally land in the United States.

A three-person committee was set up by the department head to examine his case, test his suitability for admission, and make recommendation. After the test, the committee had no doubt that Owen was eminently qualified for admission. The result of the test showed that his performance was far beyond the level expected of any student seeking admission as a freshman in the School of Architecture. He was accordingly recommended for admission in the faculty.

Owen was not only recommended for admission, he was also recommended for an award of scholarship because of his extraordinary performance in the test he took. Both recommendations were accepted by the admission authorities. In one stroke, he got what he wanted, and in addition, the problem of financing his education was solved. Owen would start his studies in September when classes begin in the fall. Meanwhile, he used the time he still had to settle and make himself ready for the work ahead.

The program in the University of Texas at Austin, School of Architecture was not much different from the one in the University of Nigeria, Nsukka, in Nigeria where Owen had completed two years of academic work before the institution was forced to close its gates because of the civil war in the country, and the students were sent away.

Owen was a mature student. He had over the years developed a habit of consistency in his work and study. He also had the discipline to utilize his time well and eliminate waste. Nothing distracted him when he set his mind at doing anything. These were the qualities of the man who was just offered an opportunity to study what he loved.

Owen did not only want to succeed; he wanted also to prove beyond all reasonable doubt that he earned the trust of the department, which did the unconventional thing of recommending his admission without seeing his prequalification papers. He felt a compelling duty to make the department feel proud and vindicated for that decision. He reminded himself that he was studying on a generous scholarship that had to be retained by excellent performance. Despite all these feelings, Owen did not do any extraordinary thing in the way he studied to always remain on top of his class. He had internalized his orderly way of doing things, including the method he approached his studies.

He was not all books. He was an excellent athlete. He played soccer, basketball, lawn and table tennis, and could swim. He, once in a while, competed in the marathon. Owen was a talented man; he exploited those talents to the fullest. There was no dull moment in his life; he was always fully engaged at anything he did at any material time. He had the ability to concentrate on whatever he did at the exclusion of other things. He was not a man to cry over spilled milk, but was always forward looking.

In the spring of 1970, Anne attended a World Conference of Humanitarian Societies in Atlanta, Georgia. She took the opportunity to visit Owen in Texas with some first-hand news from Nigeria. The civil war had ended, although there were still pockets of localized hostilities. She had actually travelled to Owen's hometown to look for members of his family. They lost four members of the extended family, which was not as bad as many families suffered. She was at pains to tell him how rapidly the situation had deteriorated in and around his hometown before the war ended, which resulted in the destruction of most of the town. His parents, she assured him, had survived, and so did his siblings.

Although Owen now knew that his parents were still alive after the 30-month civil war, it was not easy to establish any kind of communication with them, and it took another year before Owen was able to communicate with his parents. Before then, they were happy to know that Owen was still alive, and that was sufficient cause for celebration.

Back home in Owen's village, as people started to return to pick up the pieces, they learned that Bassey, as Owen was known, was alive and was going to school in America. The news brought many of the villagers some joy in the midst of the sorrows from the losses they sustained in the war. Owen was a rising star in the village, a leader among the youths. He had won many athletic competitions for the village. He was a captain of the soccer team. He sang in the church choir and performed other duties in the church. Even when he was in the university, he was still active in the activities in the village whenever he was home. Owen was the greatest hope of his family and the village.

In the university, Owen was a sensation. He did not only remain on top of his class throughout his course in the university, he also broke all the existing records in the faculty. He became the first foreign student to do so. He graduated the best all-round student in his class. There was a clear indication that he would be admitted to do a Master's program in the university.

Owen graduated on top of his class in the spring of 1974. He garnered eight of the 12 prizes awarded in the faculty, including the best overall student in academics, the best in extracurricular activities, and the best-behaved student. The lecturers who were instrumental to his admission in the university were as happy as they were stunned by his unprecedented performance.

Owen, a student who enrolled in the university in a very difficult situation and got admitted in an unusual circumstance, set a record that would be difficult to break for many years to come. He was the first foreign and first African student to do so. He became the talk of the university. For Owen, it was just the beginning of the things to come.

As was generally expected by his lecturers, Owen enrolled in the Master's program in the same department of architectural science in the summer of 1974. After the initial discussions with his supervisors, Owen started to work on his plan. It covered the areas of work the program would cover and the duration of time. In addition to his Master's program, Owen was assigned to conduct some tutorial classes for second year undergraduate students. Owen would receive some stipend for taking the students in tutorials.

Three weeks into his new assignments, Owen received two unexpected and unwanted visitors in the office complex he shared with two other post-graduate students. These men came from the United States Immigration Department. According to the men, their record showed that Owen was no longer classified as a student and was staying illegally in the United States since he had overstayed his visa. This was in fact not correct.

The visa issued to Owen would allow him to stay in the United States as long as he was a student and still studying. The expiration date of the visa simply said "duration of study," and Owen was still studying, though not as an undergraduate student. Somebody in the Immigration Department must have reckoned that, according to the records, Owen came into the country five years ago as a student, but he failed to recognize that he was still a student.

Owen was listed as one of the many foreigners who had to be deported from the country for staying illegally, having overstayed their visa. Owen was not aware of the publication until a friend of his called to intimate him; he thought it was a huge joke until the officials of the department visited the university to arrest him. Owen had no idea of what to do, but luckily for him, the incident was on a weekday, and the administration was still at work.

It took the intervention of the president of the university to stop the arrest and suspend the deportation order. The university showed proof that Owen was studying full-time in the university. It took some time for Owen to recover from the rude shock. The university's timely intervention saved him the embarrassment and another disruption in his life. The university further initiated the immigration process, as his employer, in order to grant him a permanent resident status in the United States. While that process was on, Owen was issued a work authorization permit for one year. That seemed to have temporarily closed the issue, but for Owen, it opened a whole new area of concern.

Owen was totally unaware of his visa requirement and conditions of his stay in the United Sates. His main focus was his study. He gave no thoughts to his immigration status nor did he realize that he came into the United States with a visa that could expire one day. That threat to arrest and deport him made him realize that he should be aware of other things going on in the society he lived, including the very things that affect his welfare as a resident. Although he was not out of status at the time of the threat, a mistake like that or the overzealousness of an immigration officer or even the police could cause him an irreparable harm.

To say that, before this incident, Owen had no more than a passing knowledge of the country he has lived for five years and how it worked is an understatement. He knew very little more than he knew about the country before he arrived there. He was, no doubt, devoted to his studies and lived comparably comfortable within the confines of the university environment. The incident was a wakeup call for him to get out of his shell and learn about the country he lived.

When he started, America became an entirely new world to him. He studied in-depth the history of the United States, the slave trade, the Civil War, the Declaration of Independence, and the evolution of what is now known as the United States of America. He studied the workings of the United States government, the separation of powers and the functions of each under the constitution. The more he discovered America, the more his interest became ignited. He then developed a great interest in the study of the American political, economic, and socio-cultural system.

It was during his Master's program that Owen had the opportunity to go outside Texas. The first part of the program was concentrated on course work. The second part took him outside for collection of his research materials. He visited places like the Grand Canyon in the state of Arizona, great historical sites in Florida. He realized that he had locked himself in Texas and denied himself of seeing the many wonders in America. There was no doubt that his beginning to see America other than the Lone Star State changed his thinking and attitude toward many things. He felt it was time to leave Texas and move on to somewhere else.

Owen earned his Master's degree in Architectural Science in the fall of 1975. It was an achievement that would make him consolidate his stay as a member of the university community. Just before his graduation, Owen received his permanent residency, also known as the green card. This was the best news for him after that threat by the immigration to arrest and deport him. The possession of a green card assured him that he could stay and work in the country for the next 10 years, all things being equal.

Another opportunity came when Owen was offered an employment in the university. He was offered a teaching position in the faculty where he studied. Owen unpredictably turned down the offer. His explanation was simple: he had stayed for too long in Texas and wanted to move on to somewhere else in America. Interestingly, he still remembered what Oma told him about freedom and mobility of people in America. Perhaps he wanted to put that to test.

CHAPTER SEVEN
OWEN MOVED TO MASSACHUSETTS

Owen decided on where to go from Texas after he received his green card. But first, he wanted to take a break and see some places of interest mainly along the West Coast. He would cover most of the trip by road to afford him the chance to see a lot and would also go by air where that was necessary.

Owen flew to Phoenix in Arizona and travelled over 200 miles by road to the Grand Canyon. The place captivated Owen's interest the first time he saw it. He admired the architectural wonder of nature. He saw it as a masterpiece and wanted to see it again. Owen spent three days sight-seeing and studying the Grand Canyon and its environ. He made recordings and documented the things he saw there. The scenery was not like anything he ever saw.

From the Grand Canyon, Owen flew to Los Angeles in California. Although Owen was not a film or theatre enthusiast, he wanted to visit the film city in Los Angeles. He was thrilled by what he saw in the enclave. He visited some film studios and learned a few technical things about filming and the back-stage work involved in film creation.

He would not afford the time to see all he wanted to see in the city.

He left Los Angeles, travelling north toward Sacramento, the Californian capital. He stopped over at San Luis Obispo, where he spent one night. San Luis Obispo, referred to as the happiest place in America, lies between the coastal range and the central coast wine country. Owen had enough time to visit a few of the vineyards and a few other tourist sites in the area before heading toward San Jose.

San Jose held special interest for him in a way. His main interest there was to see the Rosicrucian Park, where the grand lodge of the Ancient, Mystical Order of Rosae Crucis (AMORC) fraternity in the West is located. Owen had some remote association with the fraternity and had read a lot about it. He seized the opportunity of his visit to see many things for himself, especially in the museum with many Egyptian monuments, including miniatures of the great pyramids of Giza.

By the time Owen reached San Francisco, he felt he had seen enough to publish a tourist guide of the American cities on the Pacific coast. He saw a different picture of America from what he saw in all those years in Texas. He became better educated about America and started to seriously think of his future in America.

Owen flew from San Francisco to Portland in the state of Oregon. In Portland, he met his friend and classmate, Stanley Stevens, with whom he travelled to Salem, the capital city, and to Newport on the Pacific coast. Stanley lived in Portland with his parents. He was a brilliant student and also a keen competitor to Owen but found it difficult to beat him in class. The duo developed a mutual respect and became close friends. Besides meeting with Stanley, Owen made many new friends on the trip.

Fatigue was beginning to crop in, although Owen still had two places to go on this trip. But so far, it was all excitement and no time to rest. When he flew into Seattle in Washington State, he had only one very important place to see, that was the Boeing Factory, which was arranged for him by a tour promoter in the city. At a certain time, Owen had thought of working for Boeing. He had, however, given up that idea at the time of his visit. He still had some time to see other places, including the University of Seattle campus. There, Owen met a young Nigerian professor who tried to convince him to make a home in Seattle. Owen was always difficult to convince; his answer was that he liked to visit Seattle but not to settle there.

The last leg of his trip took him to Salt Lake City in Utah. Owen seemed to have been attracted to the city by its name more than what he expected to see. He visited the Great Salt Lake in the northwest of the city that bears its name. He also enjoyed the sight of the city's many tall buildings with their spires. Owing to the fast-deteriorating weather conditions, he could not try Mount Olympus as he originally planned. Owen, however, believed that he had seen enough on one trip. The trip lasted a good 16 days, and it was time he went to have some rest somewhere.

When Owen arrived in Boston, Massachusetts, in November, the weather was already becoming very cold for him; the second snow of the season had fallen. He has always dreaded the northeast cold weather, but now he had made up his mind to live there, so he had to learn to adapt to it. He found himself a nice one-room studio accommodation in town and settled in. He had all the time to rest and study his surroundings before he embarked on the next phase of his plan.

Owen's plan was to seek an admission and pursue a doctorate program in Harvard University. From the information he had gathered, coupled with his excellent performance in both his first degree and the Master's, he was convinced that it would not be difficult to get an admission into the College of Architecture in the university for a Ph. D degree. He was right in his conviction because it did not take too much effort; it took him one interview after he had submitted his application.

Owen had two possible courses he wanted to specialize in, one was Architectural Design and Construction Management, the other one was Architectural Design. Unfortunately for him, both were not offered in the same college. He decided to apply simultaneously to Wentworth Institute of Technology, College of Architecture Design and Construction Management in Boston and Harvard University, Graduate School of Design, Department of Architecture in Cambridge. Both colleges were close by: Cambridge was 20 minutes by road north of Boston. Owen was prepared to accept any of them that first offered him a place.

The Harvard University, Graduate School of Design in Cambridge was the first to acknowledge his application and invite him for a chat. It was a full-time program, and if everything went well, the duration would be three academic years to fulfill the requirements for an award of a Ph. D. Owen would be required to have 15 hours of teaching every week. The teaching requirement was part of the program, but he would receive appropriate full remuneration for it. If he did any additional teaching, that would be paid for separately. In addition, a reasonable cost of his approved research work would be paid by the university.

The offer was good, and Owen accepted it with pleasure. After all the nitty-gritty were sorted out, Owen met with each of the supervisors assigned to him to work out details of the program. As the details of the program showed, if all went well and accordingly, Owen would be able to complete his doctorate program by summer of 1978. Owen loved to be in Harvard University for what it was, but he could have also studied in any other renowned university in the country; and there are many of them.

It was not entirely the lure of Harvard or Massachusetts alone that made him decide to go to Harvard. By the time he finished his Master's program and decided to proceed to do his doctorate, Owen had known many architectural colleges that were as good as Harvard, if not better. He could have gone to any of them easily if he had wanted to, but he chose to go to Massachusetts to be close to Oma, the young lady he met on the plane from Paris to New York six years earlier when he came to the United States.

Owen and Oma had been in constant communication with each other since they first met, and they were developing an intimate relationship. Oma was really the reason

Owen went to Harvard; with both of them in the same city, they would see each other more frequently.

Oma was the daughter of a renowned American scientist, William Princewill. He studied in Michigan Institute of Technology before going to France to teach. He was a professor of Microbiology in the City University in Paris.

He was the reason for Oma's frequent visits to France. For the period Oma lived with her parents in France, she usually spent her summer vacations in the United States. It was during one of the flights from Paris to New York that she met Owen in the plane. Their friendship amazingly developed into an intimate relationship over the years.

Oma studied Geophysics in Massachusetts Institute of Technology in Boston. By the time Owen arrived in Massachusetts, Oma was doing her Master's program and was due to complete it in nine months. Owen and Oma saw each other frequently; their relationship metamorphosed into a courtship. The courtship did not last long when Owen proposed to Oma.

The proposal was made in an informal gathering of some friends of Owen. It was during a meeting of members of the international forum. This was a group of students in the university who met from time to time under the auspices of international students. It was not an official body in the university. Owen seized the opportunity of the gathering of the group to propose to Oma to the surprise of his friends.

Owen appeared to suddenly be in a hurry. They decided to get married in the summer of 1977. The wedding day was

August 6, 1977. It was more than the modest wedding Owen and Oma wanted. It was attended by students and professors in the academic communities of Boston and Cambridge, as well as friends outside Massachusetts. Owen's friends in New York, Texas, California, and Oregon also attended the wedding. It became a landmark event in the life of Owen since his arrival in the United States. The significance of this marriage was not lost to Owen. Oma was the first American woman Owen met and fell in love with.

Owen completed his doctorate program in the spring of 1979. It was the icing on the cake after more than nine years of sustained academic work. It was another happy moment in his life when he received the award of a doctorate degree with his wife by his side.

For a few flicking moments, his mind flashed back at a scene, only 10 years ago when Owen was pushed with the barrel of a gun to be taken to the killing field at the 16th Brigade headquarters of the Nigerian Army. He also remembered the moment he sat nervously in the plane that smuggled him to Lagos. Owen believed that the seven months he stayed in Paris as a refugee really changed his life, and he owed all to one person, Anne Dupont—and to destiny. He could not avoid thinking that he was a person of destiny; from the small village in Eastern Nigeria, now he was standing on the rostrum of one of the most renowned institutions of learning in the world, receiving acknowledgement for his achievement, not by his plans or design but through providence.

Owen found some moments alone that evening to look back into his entire life so far. He could recall that as a young man growing up, soldiering, as a profession, was never in his mind. But when his university was closed, he went for a competitive selection test as a military officer. He was one of the two selected out of 20 candidates. After his training as a cadet officer, he volunteered to be posted to the location he was as a platoon commander. One event led to another without real plans on his part.

There was only one thing he wanted: to be an academician, but the route to it was obscured by events after the civil war started and his university education was terminated. He met Oma on his first trip to the United States and maintained a relationship with her at the time relationship was not one of the things on his agenda. Destiny appeared to be at work, and he accepted it.

Owen discovered that his life was now different. He was married and knew that he could no longer take decisions without consulting with his wife and taking other factors into consideration. He had no definite plans on what to do after his postgraduate studies, though he felt he could live in Massachusetts with Oma for a while before moving to New York or Washington to explore the opportunity in the private sector.

He and Oma were still contemplating on their next move when a solution came. Owen was offered a teaching position in Harvard University, School of Design. Owen decided to accept the offer, even if it was a stop gap. Again, Owen found himself in a position he did not plan for. Teaching was an acceptable job for him, a very good starting point, and an opportunity to impact on others a subject he loved. Architecture for him was not the abstract thing people saw but a concept that affects everyday living.

Owen settled down and became fully engaged in his work. Massachusetts now became his new home; he and Oma hoped to remain there for some time. They decided that it was time to start a family. Their first child was a boy; he was born in July 1980 and was named Ben. Ben brought a lot of changes into the family. Oma had to shed off some of the work she was doing to take care of the baby, and Owen had to create time for him.

It was not long before Ben had a brother. The second child was born in August 1983. He was named Bassey. With two children to take care of, Oma stopped working completely to have enough time for them. Now within that short time, life became completely different for the couple. Their lifestyle changed. Their finances experienced some strains.

Owen started to think of leaving Boston for another state to perhaps try his hand at something different.

Owen was in good standing as an associate professor at the university when he made known his intentions to leave. He tendered his resignation and left the university in the summer of 1986. He planned to go into private business sector.

CHAPTER EIGHT
OWEN AND ASSOCIATES LLC

Owen and Associates LLC was incorporated as an architectural design company in August 1986 with its headquarters in Norfolk, Virginia. Owen was the principal partner. Oma was a director of the company in her own right. Some of the other partners included two former classmates of Owen and two friends in New York. The company was fitted to handle management, design, construction, research, and consultation.

The company registered as major government and defense industry establishment contractor. It began to advertise heavily and engaged a lobbying company for job procurement. The result was instant success. The company won many public design and construction jobs.

The major breakthrough came when the company won a highly competitive contract to design a ship for the navy for operation in the Mediterranean Sea. It was the one job that put Owen and Associates on top and made it a reference point among defense industry contractors.

The company performed extremely well in the few years of its existence. The two branch offices in Pennsylvania and Oklahoma were doing well, too, and were almost independent in operational matters. Owen had to reduce the frequency of his visits to the branch offices.

Meanwhile, Oma had a third child in December 1987. It was another boy who got the name Dan. By now, Ben was seven and in school. Bassey was four years old. With the growing family, Oma had to reduce her time with the company. Even for Owen, he had to delegate most of the duties that often took him out of Norfolk.

Owen and Associates LLC attained a national status as a public establishment contractor and leading member of defense industry contractors. It was expanding to become self-sufficient and gradually cutting down on the outside companies to which it was outsourcing some functions and supplies. With its geographical expansion to the Midwest and West Coast, its workforce increased exponentially.

It was the westward expansion of the activities of the company that made Owen consider moving to Oklahoma. The movement would involve only his personal staff while Norfolk would continue to remain the company's headquarters. A decision was taken that Owen would move to Oklahoma in the fall of 1991.

On February 12, 1991, Oma gave birth to her forth child, this time a girl. She was given the name Mabel, after Oma's mother who had passed on a few years earlier. Later in the year Owen, Oma with their four children, would leave Norfolk.

Owen and Oma with their four children arrived in Oklahoma in September 1991. The first duty was to settle the family in the new environment. Mabel was only seven months old, and Dan was four years. Ben was 11, Bassey was eight, and both of them were in school. Oma's schedule did not change much; she spent much of her time taking care of the children and only occasionally had to put in a few hours of consulting work for the company where her expertise was needed.

The family settled fast in their new home and life went on smoothly. As Owen had anticipated, the company was growing fast in the Midwest and on the West Coast. He was making visits to California and Seattle from time to time to meet some clients. Through hard work, foresight, effective leadership ,and harmony in the workplace Owen and Associates LLC grew into a formidable organization.

Owen was beginning to believe and boast that America was the place where one could fulfill his destiny when the event of May 3, 1999, occurred and shattered his plans. Going by his experience, Owen has weathered many storms, but what happened on that day was enough to destroy him. Owen counted it as part of the burden he was meant to bear.

May 3, 1999, was a Monday, and everybody who had to work was at work. The first hint of any danger on that day came after 12:00 noon in a public alert of a likely tornado that evening. The confirmation of a coming tornado was made later that afternoon at about 4:15 PM, and a red alert was issued. People living in the Oklahoma area and the environs were advised to remain indoors possibly in secure basements in the anticipation of a strong tornado that was forecast to hit parts of the state that evening.

Owen, like many other citizens, heeded the warning and hurried back home from work. Back home, Owen called Ben and Bassey. Ben, who was then 19, was in the university away from home. Bassey, who was 16 and in his senior high school year, was also away from home. Both of them were expected back home in another five weeks. Owen was at home with Oma and the other two children, Dan and Mabel. The tornado warning was still on when, at about 7:00PM, Owen remembered that he had to pick up a prescription drug from a pharmacy just few minutes away. Five minutes later, Owen was in the pharmacy when the tornado struck.

Owen spent the next two hours in the basement of the pharmacy with the workers and other customers, who like him were forced to stay there for their safety. At that moment, Owen thought less of his safety than his family's and made several attempts to leave, but it was physically impossible to walk on the street. Heavy rain followed the tornado. The streets were blocked by fallen trees and debris from destroyed houses. The city was plunched into darkness.

The tornado hit southeast Oklahoma City, where Owen lived, the hardest, reaching a speed of 115 miles per hour (185 kilometers per hour). Everything on its path was destroyed or swept away. The entire area laid waste, especially the southern and eastern parts of Oklahoma City and the suburbs of Bridge Creek, Moore, Del City, Mideast City, and Tucker Air Force Base.

When Owen finally left the pharmacy and ventured out, it was past 9:00 that evening. The roads were blocked by falling trees, electric poles, tangled electric wires, and debris from falling houses. The streets were dark, and it was still raining. It was difficult to move, and he picked his way slowly not knowing how long it would take to get to the house.

It was difficult for Owen to locate where his house was; there were no landmarks anymore, and the streets were covered in darkness. There was no single house still standing on his street. After identifying his street, he had to do some calculation to locate the point where his house stood before. His two-story, six bedroom house had been reduced to a heap of crushed bricks and steel. The mangled roof lay some 100 yards across the street. And there was no single life in sight. From what he saw, the street was on the direct path of the tornado.

Owen knew from instinct, and from what he saw, that his wife and two children were lying under the debris. In his confusion and disorientation, he tried to pull the debris with his bare hands in an attempt, he thought, to rescue them. He was helpless; there was nobody to contact, nowhere to seek help, and nowhere to go. He sat down on the debris, as if he was keeping watch over his wife and children under it. Overcome with grief and the hostile elements of the night, Owen passed out still sitting on top of the ruins of his former house. Later that night, he was picked up by a passing rescue team and taken to an emergency clinic where he spent the dreadful night.

Owen woke up the following morning, wondering how he got to the hospital where he found himself. Gradually, he started to remember the events of the previous evening leading to the time he traced his way to where his house had been. It then occurred to him that his wife and children might not have survived if they were still under the debris for those past hours. He started asking questions, discharged himself from the hospital, and called his office for help. His office was in the part of town not affected by the tornado, though some of the workers who lived outside that zone were affected.

His efforts were now focused on how to get people to rescue his family. The rescuers had their hands full, even with help from the neighboring states and federal agencies. His office had to provide the equipment and men to help Owen. By the time the team could work their way through the heap of steel and bricks to the basement of the house, it was late in the afternoon, and it had been 20 hours since the tornado hit the city.

It was a moment of shock and grief. The three bodies of mother and two children were pulled out under the weight of a collapsing wall as they were moving into the basement of the house. The mother was still grasping the telephone. Dan was 12, and Mabel eight years old. Owen almost passed out.

Owen knew that natural disasters have been with us as long as human beings have walked the Earth and have occurred in America as long as we can remember, but it does not seem to mean much to some people until it affects them. Owen did not think much about the tornado when the warning was posted. He had lived through many natural disasters since he arrived in the United States 30 years ago. But when he looked at the three bodies in front of him, the reality of the havoc of natural disasters stared him in the face. He wished he was dreaming.

The deadly tornado that took the lives of Oma, Dan and Mabel, and many others in Oklahoma on May 3, 1999, was, by then, the second most costly in the United States history. More than 8,000 homes were destroyed or damaged; the cost in dollar terms was $1.4 billion. Fifty people were reported killed across three states—Oklahoma, Southern Kansas, and North Texas. Most of the destruction occurred in Oklahoma.

Owen had been married for 22 years. For all those years, their relationship as husband and wife was enviable. It seemed to have been a perfect union. Oma was a piece of eye candy, and Owen was the kind of man any woman would want in her life. They had four children who were brought up in the image of their parents. The death of Oma and the two children was the most devastating thing in Owen's life, but as a man who believed in destiny, he viewed it philosophically. He could not come to terms with events of that evening.

Why did he have to leave the house at that particular time the tornado struck? He has been home for more than three hours before that time, and did not remember to go to pick up his prescription drug in the pharmacy. Was it to spare his life? Why was his life spared and that of his wife and children taken away? Could he have done anything to save their lives if he was home? Was there any consideration of the two children who were in school? Who did this calculation to let him live with the two boys and to be able to bury the wife and the other children?

Why did those three have to die at all, for what purpose? These were few of the questions Owen asked himself, but as a believer, he did not want to fault his God. He accepted the situation and was ready to move on.

The funeral of Oma, Dan, and Mabel took place on May 15, 12 days after the event. It was about the last of the series of funerals round the city. It was a solemn occasion attended by a mammoth crowd of people from different walks of life, including friends and colleagues from Massachusetts, Pennsylvania, Texas, Norfolk, and New York. Ben and Bassey arrived from school one day before to be by their father's side and share the grief of the passing of their beloved mother and siblings. They returned to school after the ceremony to finish the school year.

After the funeral, Owen was all alone to absorb the impact of the deaths. It was a very difficult time for him; a time to take a hard look at the situation and make a decision about his future. After days of deep contemplation, Owen came to the conclusion that his journey and American chapter of his life has come to an end. He was now considering how to pull himself together and go back to where he always called home. Luckily for him, he had been home twice in the last 12 years. He owned a house in the town. Owen would not be a total stranger in his home. Going home now was more than a mere wish.

Owen had lived in the United States for 30 years. He loved each day of those 30 years. He also knew from the beginning that America was not his home, that one day he would go back to the home he left hurriedly in a circumstance he did not choose. But it never crossed his mind that it would happen the way it did. He always said and would always remember that America was a good host to him and would not have wished anything better until that fateful day he lost his beloved wife and children to an act of God.

The actualization of this decision presented him with a daunted human problem. It meant abandoning the relationships he had built and cultivated in 30 years, and divesting in a business empire he established and painstakingly nurtured to bring to that enviable level. Although Owen was born in Nigeria, his entire productive life was spent in the United States. His enormous wealth was in the United States. Most of his friends and associates were in the United States. What going back home meant was to go and start a new life without a family, without friends, and without his economic base. Owen realized the enomity of his decision but would not change his mind. He was now looking at a future across the Atlantic.

His immediate attention was to discuss and decide the fate of the company. As the CEO and Chairman of the Board of Directors of the company, Owen called a meeting of the Executive Directors and Board members of Owen and Associates LLC to inform the members of his decision so that they could decide the future of the company without him. Owen had decided to divest completely from the company as a majority shareholder. He would, however, recommend that his sons, Ben Owen and Bassey Owen, be taken on board as Directors. The shares held by their late mother would be transferred to them, so each of them would have 50 percent of the total. Keeping the name of the company, which he believed was good for business, was purely the decision of the board members.

Owen reckoned that it would take some months for everything to be worked out before he left the country. The children had to be settled, too, in a place of their choice since Owen was going back alone. By his calculation, end of the year might be an appropriate time to leave. He began sorting out his personal affairs to be able to meet this dateline. He believed he would be able to tidy up and finally leave by third week of December. He chose this time when he could slip in quietly while the Christmas festivities were going on in the city. He knew that Christmastime at home was a time of festivities when everybody was concerned with having a good time. Besides, it was the time of year when most people living outside the state would go home. He would arrive and slip into the city without attracting any special attention.

The tidying up of his affairs was harder than Owen thought at first. He had to go through volumes of paper work to sift out things he needed for his future work. He travelled quite a lot to many cities to meet personally with people to discuss variety of issues, many of them in connection with the severance from his company and others in connection with his future plans.

By the middle of June, Ben and Bassey were at home with their father to begin the long summer vacation. Ben would go back to Harvard in September, and Bassey would join him as a freshman in the same university but in a different faculty. It was the time for the father to fill them with what they did not know about the May 3 deaths of their mother and siblings. It was the time for the father to brief them about many other things. They needed to know much about the family, especially now their father had decided to go back to Nigeria and leave them alone on their own in the United States. They were not just visitors as their father used to refer to himself; they were citizens.

For some time, Ben and Bassey would live together in Boston, Massachusetts, in a house purchased and paid for by their father until they decided on what to do and how to live their lives in the future. In another two years, Bassey would be 18 years old; Ben, who was already 19, would officially be Bassey's guardian. Owen assured them that everything would be fine while he would be away.

Everything worked out as he planned; Owen would be leaving the United States for good on December 17, 1999, seven months after he lost his wife and two children in that deadly tornado. At 51, he believed that he would still be able to start all afresh at home and get to the height he always dreamed of. He had already decided on what to do when he got home. He knew that with some adjustment to suit the economic and social environment, he would function properly and profitably.

Owen had gotten the important tools he would need to take off in business. He would not depend on any financial assistance from the bank that may limit what he had in mind; the capital would come from the proceeds of the sale of his shares in his former company. It was substantial and ran into hundreds of millions of dollars. In his calculation, he would be financially self-sustained for many years before any expected income. With this mind set and arrangements made, and all things being equal, Owen did not intend to waste one single day when he arrived home.

Meanwhile, his friends and former associates were falling heads over heels in calling to arrange social meetings to bid Owen farewell. Owen had a hard time declining the invitations from most of them because, as he said, he wanted to leave as quietly as he came in. He, however, made himself available to them but not in a social gathering. He did not want to antagonize anyone, believing that he might need them some day.

Many of his friends who met or spoke to Owen tried to make him feel sorry for wanting to leave the United States at a time he was on top of the socio-economic ladder. His company was one of the best performing companies in its class. It enjoyed the competitive edge it had among the defense contractors. The company's profit continued to rise year after year. None of these were able to convince Owen to change his mind. But he knew that he would from time to time come to America for something or just on a visit; after all he was leaving his sons behind in the country.

CHAPTER NINE
THE RETURN JOURNEY

One thing was sure. It was not the loss of his wife and children that made Owen decide to leave the United States of America for his home in Nigeria. From the first day he arrived in the United States, Owen knew that he was in the country as a guest and a visitor. It did not matter how long he stayed and how good things were going for him, he would go back to his roots.

The loss of his wife and children might have been an awakening signal, a reminder that it was time to move. He saw it as the time to leave the scene and go to start a new chapter. Owen recalled many times over the years the manner circumstances made him leave his country. He was reduced to a position of helplessness. Each time he remembered that moment, Owen felt bad inspite of his accomplishment. Leaving the United States was his choice, his decision, and his responsibility.

Owen had turned down all proposals by his friends who wanted to see him off at the airport; only Ben and Bassey accompanied him to the airport that evening. It was the same airport through which he first entered the

United States 30 years ago, but this time, JFK in New York had no excitement for him, nor the expectancy it had then. The excitement of going home finally after the many long and eventful years was subdued. The only show of emotion was when he bid his children farewell and walked the security area to his waiting plane.

The Air France flight he boarded in New York would take him to Charles de Gaulle's airport in Paris, where he would change to another Air France flight and fly to Lagos, Nigeria, the following day. This was the same route, the same airline he used 30 years ago, and to Owen, it seemed as if he was tracing his way back to where he came from. The layover time in Paris would be six hours, and Owen intended to use this time to meet his long-time friend, Anne Dupont.

From his first-class seat, Owen looked down one last time to have a glimpse of New York City. It was beautiful, he thought, and suddenly, the realization came that it was not the last time he would see New York. The fun memory of the city and indeed the entire country spontaneously awakened in him. He, however, wanted to forget it at that moment and move on.

A few minutes into the flight, as the plane gained altitude and stabilized, Owen put up the "do not disturb" sign, leaned back on his seat, and dosed off. He was really tired and needed some rest badly. The last 48 hours were hectic for him; streams of visitors and endless telephone calls gave him no opportunity to enjoy the luxury of sleep. He admitted all visitors and accepted all calls but turned down all wishes to see him off at the airport. He thought his two children were enough company.

Owen woke up after two hours of sleep and felt re-freshed. A flight attendant was at hand to serve him some refreshment and dinner. He then spent the next few hours reading a book he picked at the airport book stall—a book he had always wanted to read—*The Exodus* by Leon Uris. He was still reading when the pilot announced preparation for landing. The plane landed at 5:30 AM local time. After the immigration formalities, Owen went to the VIP lounge to wait for his flight connection. He had six hours lay-over time. He had planned to meet Anne during the time. Anne turned up at 8:00.

Anne, now Madame Anne Dupont, married with three children, was in her early sixties. She had been a friend of Benjamin Owen for 31 years. She stopped working for Medicins Sans Frontieres 15 years ago. They met in the airport restaurant for breakfast.

Anne and Benjamin were no strangers to each other. They discussed almost everything under the sun, except by mutual consent, the misfortune for which Owen was still grieving. They revisited the moment of their first meeting in Port Harcourt, Nigeria, in 1968 and sub-sequent events in Owen's life since then. Anne was still the only person Owen could freely discuss his life. The meet-ing was very refreshing for both of them. And by the time they said goodbye to each other, Owen was ready to board his connecting flight to Lagos.

It was another Air France flight that would take Owen and other passengers to Lagos. It took off at 11:30 AM local time and was scheduled to take five and a half hours. Immediately the plane reached a stabilizing altitude,

Owen put up the "do not disturb" sign and slept off. By the time he woke up, the plane was flying over the sahara desert and it would be in Lagos in another three hours.

Owen recalled that he did not inform anybody of his homecoming and so did not expect any person to receive him on arrival. He knew Lagos well and had booked his hotel accommodation for the number of days he intended to stay in the city before flying to his home state capital, 500 miles (800 kilometers) east of Lagos, his final destination.

As the plane moved steadily toward its destination, Owen allowed himself a little pleasure of reminiscing on how it was 31 years ago in November 1968 when he departed Lagos for Paris with a small suitcase containing all his earthly possessions. Now he was returning to Lagos with eight suitcases. Then nobody saw him off, and now, nobody would receive him. He also knew that a lot of things have changed, he left as a 20-year-old young man full of dreams, which seemed to have temporarily halted and now he was returning a 51-year-old man with renewed dreams. For all those years, he had been shown kindness, and he reciprocated in kind. Will his society show him that same kindness now that he was back home, he rhetorically asked.

Many other things crossed Owen's mind as the plane was landing. For the first time, he wondered if he would have survived the war in the circumstance he was to be able to pick up the pieces again. Might be he would have survived and might be the war would have completely transformed him as it did to so many people. He was sure, he told himself, that he would not have been the same person who was now coming back home for good. The landing of the plane cut off further thoughts and brought Owen to full awareness. He was now in Lagos international airport, Ikeja.

Owen went through the immigration formalities with little problem but spent two very uncomfortable hours to collect his luggage. The air-condition system in the airport had broken down, and he labored under an unbearable heat to get his luggage from a manually-operated conveyor belt. That was not a kind welcome but simply a sign of the things to see at home. The taxi took 90 minutes from the airport to the hotel, a distance of 16 kilometers (10 miles). By the time Owen reached the hotel, it was 10;30 PM. For a flight that landed at 5:45 PM local time, that was unimaginable. Owen, however, heaved a sigh of relief because it could have been worse if he had missed any of his luggage, which was not an uncommon and daily experience of passengers arriving at the airport.

The hotel was quite a contrast to the chaos at the airport and on the road. The receptionists were kind and humane; the rooms were comfortable; the environment was serene; and the entire atmosphere was inviting. It seemed to have belonged to a different world. It provided the little comfort Owen so very badly needed. Owen spent three days in Lagos.

His stay in Lagos was not just a break on his journey, he wanted to establish contacts with some business people he would need in connection with the business he intended to start as soon as he got home. Owen was considering registering an architectural company as a major

concern and one or two subsidiary companies simultaneously. The few contacts he made were invited to his
hotel room for discussions that he found very useful. As
an intended newcomer into the Nigerian business space,
he believed that he needed to discuss with people who had
been on the scene for some time, and there was no better
place to do that than in Lagos.

○   ○   ○

After three days, Owen left Lagos. The flight to his home
state took one hour. It took another 30 minutes to pick up
his luggage. He did not fail to notice the different atmosphere at the airport in Calabar where he landed. Everything was orderly; Owen could feel the friendliness in
the air.

Owen had hoped to land incognito, but it turned out
not to be the case. He forgot that he grew up in that town
and still had friends who might recognize him. Although
they were at the airport on their own business, two of
Owen's boyhood friends recognized him and went to meet
him. Before he knew it, there was a crowd around and
chatting with him. They all remembered him as Bassey.
Owen did not need to hire any taxi. He was given a free
ride into town, straight to his hotel. Owen's house, which
had remained unoccupied for the last three years, had to
be cleaned first before he could move in.

Owen recalled his thoughts while he was in the plane;
perhaps this gesture by his friends of decades ago was the
beginning of the kindness he expected from the society.

After all, he thought, the society might not have changed that much, since one could still find people who would spare their time and resources to offer unsolicited help to somebody they had not met for a long time and somebody they may not expect any return favor. Owen might have jumped to conclusion because his contact with people in the coming weeks proved to be completely different. He knew better that a sparrow does not make a summer.

The Nigerian society had changed a lot more than he thought. There was a complete change in values. Socio-economic changes made money the only thing people craved for; how they got it did not matter, and nobody seemed to ask any questions. Discipline had completely broken down in the society that many parents were unable to keep their children under any control. The new geo-political changes after the civil war created new orientations and loyalties. Everything seemed to have been monetized, including morality in the society. The congestion in the city caused by population drift from the villages was part of the change and the most visible one. There were hordes of young people roaming the streets trying to eke out a living or to steal what they could.

He was really concerned with what he saw. The socio-economic situation was so bad that only the high-handedness and the brutality of the police prevented a complete breakdown of law and order. His surprise was perhaps more in the fact that the authorities appeared unwilling or unable to do anything or not knowing what to do to change the situation than in the actual existence of the situation.

What Owen saw was actually a tip of the iceberg. Politics seemed to be the only thing that mattered. It became the source of ill-gotten wealth. By it, the society was exploited and rendered impotent. Politicians moved around with thugs they called bodyguards. They drove the finest automobiles in town and lived in secured areas in the city. For the others, the constant battlecry was insecurity of life and property. They were trapped in the cycle of poverty and insecurity.

Owen did not see anything wrong in change; after all, the only thing that is constant in the world is change. But what he saw was disorder and chaos in the society and a deep divide between the neglected many and the favored few. As the saying goes, a government that cannot provide for the many who are poor would be unable to protect the few who are rich. This was the society Owen saw as he came back home and prepared to settle in.

Owen saw what many people could not see in that society. He did not see just the chaos and disorder and a disgruntled population; he also saw solution to these ills. There were enormous opportunities for investment in the society. There was so much work to get the youths off the road and gainfully employed. What appeared to be lacking was the ability to harness the abundant resources for a productive society. Owen believed that he would make a difference using the resources and the experience he had.

CHAPTER TEN
HOME SWEET HOME

Owen spent the first few weeks at home studying the investment terrain vis-à-vis the economic situation and making preparations to start some business. He consulted widely with people in the private sector as well as those in the public sector. He had already decided to invest in two critical areas. He incorporated "Owen & Associates Architectural Design" as a limited liability company. Although he had the resources to meet the required capital, he had to bring in two junior partners to meet the requirement of the law. His father was also designated a non-executive director of the company.

The new company started operations at a temporary location in two rooms on the ground floor of Owen's house. The first job handled by the company was the design and construction of its headquarters building. It was a magnificent edifice that changed the landscape in many ways; it became a landmark in the city. Apart from providing office space for Owen & Associates Architectural Design, the complex was designed to have shops and offices and a large car park. The construction took 10 months to complete, working seven days a week.

Owen was determined to bring his theory of how good architecture can lead to a positive social change in people and the society. He worked on it in the United States and saw the successful effects, and he thought, it could also work in his home. His office structure and car park were the first imposing projects in the area. They became a landmark in the city. He planned two small housing projects with separate and independent infrastructure for middle class dwellers. He wanted to make them models of how people should live a modest comfortable life.

The greatest tool Owen had in the development of the company was his American experience. Owen had to develop his manpower, change the attitude of workers from work as a means of getting paid every month to commitment to work. He started a crusade to change people's work ethics. His employees changed from the work-can-go-to-hell attitude as long as I can get my pay. It was not long before words spread that there was a company that paid and treated workers very well but would fire workers without notice if they did not perform.

Owen started the company with 10 permanent workers. Two of them were professionals with university degrees in architecture, four had some working experience in related fields, and four of the 10 had no work experience at all. Owen was prepared to teach and train them into what he wanted workers to be. To him, hard work, loyalty, and commitment were the prerequisites to development and success in the work place, and that was what he demanded and got from his workers. The company in return provided for the workers' welfare and paid them more than living wages. This was Owen's formula for success in his business. The people who helped to create the wealth, should also be able to enjoy part of the wealth.

As business activities expanded, the company's workforce increased accordingly. In two years' operation, the workforce reached more than 300, well-trained and motivated. Owen's success and fast growth in his business was partly attributed to the commitments of his workers and the value the company placed on them.

Meanwhile, Owen also decided to incorporate a finance company to perform mainly two functions. The major function of the finance company was to loan money to small business people and traders, mainly women at a low interest rate. Besides, no collaterals were needed to take a loan. The only condition was to identify the business the applicant was engaged in and the ability to repay the loan. The company officials also examined the viability of their business and offered advice. The second function was to accept savings from small business people and traders at a higher interest rate than commercial banks. It was Owen's form of socio-economic assistance to people in the lower income bracket.

The purpose of the establishment of this finance company by Owen was to help the small businessperson and traders who could not afford to borrow money from the commercial banks for their businesses. The complex procedure and high interest rates charged by commercial banks made it absolutely impossible for these groups of investors and traders to raise money for their businesses. The finance company did not function like a conventional bank, because it was not. Its interest rate on loans was much lower, and its interest on savings was much higher than in the commercial banks. The operation of the company was simplified, and it needed few workers to handle the daily business transactions of customers.

The finance company was an instant success. Many branches opened in the city and in some big villages. Small businesses expanded, economic activities blossomed, and the lives of many in the communities saw a positive change, especially that of the women. They were able to put away small sums of money they did not need immediately in the bank for some interest. The banking culture was extended to those who were hitherto excluded.

It was not long before the public started to notice the rise of Benjamin Owen as a special kind of businessman and his contribution to his community. Apart from what his finance company was doing to the people, he offered sponsorship to needy students in tertiary institutions. Owen's scholarship scheme became institutionalized, and many students were looking forward to it every year. Many people in the community owed their education to the generosity of Benjamin Owen.

The name Benjamin Owen soon became synonymous with humanitarianism. He never turned away any person or group that sought his assistance. Communities, as well as individuals, sought his assistance. He provided clean water, electricity, and paved roads to many communities and helped to improve their standard of living. He became a household name in the community; many youths would aspire to be like him. One person caught his attention in one of the communities. He was Colonel James.

Colonel James, Owen recalled, was the commander of the army brigade where Owen spent four months in "captivity," constantly threatened to be executed before he escaped to Lagos. That was 34 years earlier. When Owen met Colonel James again, he had retired from the military; he was no longer that man of pomposity and braggadocio. The source of his power and authority had gone with his retirement. He now lived as a normal human being in a real world. The change in his lifestyle and years of struggling had taken a great toll on him. Age and hardship were also telling on him.

The old war horse wanted to start a relationship with Owen based on the former relationship 34 years earlier. Owen, on the other hand, refused to make any reference, either in words or in action, to that relationship. Owen wanted to treat Colonel James like any other person who needed his assistance, but because of his persistence in asking, he got more than he deserved.

Society seemed to have forgotten Colonel James; even his own very constituency abandoned him. He remained an unsung, unrewarded "hero." Owen found him, lifted him up, and gave him a chance to live again. But surprisingly, he was insatiable. He told all those who cared to listen, how he saved Owen's life and wanted to portray him as an ingrate. But the people knew better. Deep down in him, Owen always knew that Colonel James did not have the powers he ascribed to himself to be able to take Owen's life. Owen had witnessed hundreds of innocent people being condemned to death by the order of this man. Owen, being the kind of man he was, did not want the man's past fiendish behavior to stop his magnanimity toward him.

Owen survived the ordeal he was subjected to by Colonel James because of his unshaken belief and trust in his God and in himself as a man of destiny. He was a deeply religious person but avoided ostentatious religious practices. His strength lay in absolute confidence in himself to seek for and get what he needed, and the commitment to serve others and humanity. He believed in serving God through service to humanity.

Owen seldom discussed his past life with people except with his children and his wife when she was alive. It was not that he was ashamed of anything he did in the past, but he grew up to be a man who always lived in the present and focused in the future. To him, the past was simply a reference point referred to when needed to guide events in the future. Owen's present focus was on the growth and development of his business empire and how he could contribute to the welfare and development of the people in his society, the place he always called home. He was beginning to see the results of his efforts and was happy about it.

Owen got a shock one morning as he arrived at work. His accountant brought to his attention an anomaly she spotted in the account of the company. The account reflected a deficit of 420 million naira (about $2.2 million). That was enough to cripple the company's activities. Owen wasted no time; he and the accountant went to see the bank manager. After a protracted discussion, the manager informed Owen that the problem could only be resolved at the bank's headquarters in Lagos and advised him to personally go there.

Owen was in Lagos the following day. After examining his account, the bank manager referred Owen to his brokerage agency, where he said the mistake originated. A few weeks earlier, Owen had decided to raise some money for further expansion of his business, and he instructed his broker to sell 30 percent of his holdings in two companies. According to the broker, the amount raised from the transaction was 420 million naira but nobody, neither the bank nor the broker, could explain why Owen's company account was debited instead of being credited.

The issue became more complex than Owen thought at first. He simply wanted his account reversed. From the bank's point of view, the 420 million naira represented a loan to his company, though no request was made for any loan, and none was granted. The bank demanded interest on the amount. Owen made a counter claim that he had to be paid interest for the period he was deprived of the use of the money. However, in order to resolve the problem, Owen was prepared to forfeit his claim if the other party would do the same and credit his account.

Instead, a further complication developed. The problem was now viewed as a case of fraud, and to start with, the account had to be frozen. Owen did not know what to make out of this; the two days he planned to stay in Lagos had run out. It was now a legal issue, and Owen was involved as a witness. Owen sought a legal advice. He would sue both his broker firm and the bank for fraudulently depriving him from the use of his money and would seek remedy. It became a ding-dong legal battle that kept Owen for another two days in Lagos.

The parties finally reached an agreement out of court with the help of their lawyers. Owen would be paid interest on his 420 million naira for the period the money had been in the bank, and the bank would unfreeze his account immediately.

Owen wanted to leave Lagos immediately, but he had no money to settle his hotel bills and purchase a ticket that had to be paid for in cash. He went to the bank to get some money, but his account was still frozen. After pleading with the manager to no avail, Owen decided to go back to the hotel and wait until his account could be accessed. It was already a Friday, which meant that Owen would spend the weekend in Lagos, doing nothing.

As Owen was about to leave the bank, a young lady, a senior bank officer, accosted him. He hesitated and then turned to face the lady. Owen could not hide his admiration of what he saw; the lady was tall and elegant with long black hair and exceptional blue eyes for a black woman. Besides the captivating beauty before him, Owen also saw the striking resemblance in physical appearance between him and the lady. Owen, trim and elegant, stood at six feet two inches; the beautiful lady was nearly as tall. Both of them would easily stand out in a crowd. They were instantly drawn to each other like magnet. She addressed Owen as Mr. Bassey and apologized that she overheard what he was discussing with the bank manager.

"My name is Blessing. It appears, Mr. Bassey, that you need some help."

"Thank you, Blessing. Yes, you're right, I need some help. And how can you help me?"

Blessing knew that Owen was her kinsman; apart from sharing a name, there were other things about him she saw but could not explain. The urge to speak to him was so intense that she could not subdue it. His need for some money became a perfect excuse.

"I know you don't live in Lagos, and you want to get back home. If you need some money, I can be of help. How much do you need?"

Owen knew that there was no need prolonging the conversation and arguing with the young lady who was ready and offered to help him.

"Thank you, Blessing, I should need enough money to take me home and a little more to settle my hotel bills, say a 100,000 naira"

"If you can wait for me," said Blessing, "I'll be back with the money in no time." She hurried away.

Owen could not comprehend; this was a young lady, a perfect stranger, he thought, who offered to help him in a society where entrusting friends with money was rare. As he was still struggling to make some sense out of it, the lady returned with an envelope and handed it to Owen.

"This is 100,000 naira, sir."

"Thank you, Blessing," said Owen, as he took the envelope, held it as if it was the most prized thing in his life. "I appreciate what you've done for me. How do I pay back the money?"

The lady managed a smile and told him, "My name is Blessing Okon Bassey, and here is my account number. Please pay it into this account when you get to Calabar."

Owen looked at the lady in astonishment and tried very hard to hide his surprise. He recalled that his former names were Bassey Okon Bassey before he changed his names to Benjamin Bassey Owen. He quickly overcame the shock and put the name sharing to a co-incidence. After all, these were common names in the area. Still fumbling, he managed to say, "What a small world. Please call me Benjamin Bassey Owen." He thanked Blessing again and hurried out of the bank. It was already 11:00, and the next flight to Calabar was at 2:30 PM. He knew that the traffic to the airport was unpredictable, even at that time of the day.

Throughout the one-hour duration of the flight from Lagos to Calabar, Owen found it difficult to think of other things. He continued to see Blessing, her beauty, her elegance, and her steadfast look at Owen. For the first time in many years since Owen came back, he saw a woman who made him start to think of women again. He was sure that it was not the last time he would see Blessing. Owen remembered the look in the lady's eyes that first time they met and knew that their meeting was not so accidental.

Early on Monday following his arrival from Lagos, Owen dutifully sent somebody from his office to the First Bank branch in Calabar to pay 100,000 naira into Blessing's bank account. He called her thereafter to let her know that her account had been credited and to thank her again. It was also an opportunity for Owen to speak to her, referring to her intimately as "my beautiful angel," and he asked her to let him know if there was anything he could do for her in Calabar. It was the beginning of a relationship.

Contrary to what Owen would admit, since the brief meeting with Blessing in Lagos, his emotional life changed drastically. He would from time-to-time start thinking about Blessing; his thoughts would momentarily drift away from his work into a brown study and suddenly would come out of it. It was during one of those moments that his telephone rang. The call came from Blessing. It was one month after Owen came back from Lagos.

Blessing called to inform Owen that she would be visiting Calabar on an official duty for one week and requested Owen to make a hotel reservation for her. Owen noted a coincidence, that Blessing called at the very time he, Owen, was thinking about her. He also concluded that Blessing wanted to see him again; otherwise, her office in Calabar could have conveniently made a hotel reservation for her since she was coming on an official duty. But Blessing chose to ask Owen to do so as a way of notifying him of her coming. That was Owen's deduction from that action. It was right, and as they say, one thing led to another.

He was, however, delighted that he would be able to see Blessing again earlier than he expected and would be able to use the opportunity of her visit to reciprocate the kind gesture she showed him in Lagos. He made the hotel reservation in her name, paid the required deposit, and instructed the hotel that all the bills would be settled by him.

At a certain point, Owen thought he could offer to accommodate her in his house, and almost called to suggest so, but after some consideration, he decided to respect her request and keep the reservation. Besides, Owen thought that she might not be comfortable to stay with him since she did not know him much nor did she have the knowledge that he had no family in the house. So, he left the matter hanging until her arrival, when Owen believed that a situation might arise when the suggestion may come naturally. Owen lived in a very comfortable five-bedroom mansion with himself and two younger relations as the only occupants; there was enough provision for visitors in the house.

Owen was anxiously looking forward to the date of Blessing's arrival. He kept that day free and spent the time at home. Usually, Owen did not go to the airport to receive visitors, whether personal or official. It was customary, as a company policy, for Owen to send drivers to the airport to meet and bring in visiting guests, but Owen decided to go to the airport to receive Blessing himself instead of sending a driver.

O O O

On the day Blessing arrived, the weather was fine, the unpredictable rain had stopped two hours earlier, and the sun was gradually coming out. Owen drove the 25 minutes to the airport with anxiety and anticipation, the kind of feeling he never had for a very long time. He worried if he would recognize her in the usual flood of passengers from a Lagos flight. He tried to recall her face, her elegant features, and her beautiful smile, and reassured himself that he would not miss her.

He was at the airport long before the plane arrived and took a conspicuous position from where he had a command view of the single gate, which all the passengers would pass through. The plane arrived in time, and within minutes of its arrival, passengers started to stream into the arrival hall. It was not long before Owen saw a tall, gorgeously dressed woman Owen recognized as Blessing. She walked with majestically measured steps. As Owen started moving toward her, their eyes met, and a smile lighted her face. Owen missed a heartbeat. There was no mistake; she was indeed his Blessing.

"Blessing," Owen called with a return smile and raising his voice as if he was not sure who she was.

"Good afternoon, Dr. Bassey," Blessing greeted, preferring to address Owen by the name that reminded her of the father she never knew. "Thank you for coming to receive me."

"You are welcome to Calabar," Owen replied. "I hope you enjoyed your flight."

As Owen stretched one hand to take Blessing's hand luggage and the other hand to give her a hand shake, Blessing ignored it and instead opened her arms in a warm embrace. Owen responded and kissed her on the cheek. The welcome ceremony was complete, and they moved toward the parking lot.

Blessing was surprised to see that Owen drove the car himself to the airport to meet her. It was the usual practice that people of his socio-economic standing in the society would send a driver to pick up their guests from the airport. She did not mention her observation in their conversation but simply noted it. Maybe, she thought, Owen wanted to have a personal relationship with her.

On the way into town, Owen asked Blessing if she really needed to stay in a hotel, that he could offer her a place in his house if she would accept to stay there. Blessing asked Owen to take the decision and count on her to abide with whatever decision he took. The two acted as if they were already lovers, Owen "announced" that the decision was that she was not going to the hotel. They both applauded the wise decision.

The drive from the airport took only 30 minutes. Blessing was shown into the guest quarters on the first floor. It comprised of a bed-room and a living room. Owen had instructed the place to be made ready for occupation in anticipation that Blessing would agree to come to the house, as it indeed happened.

As Owen led Blessing into the room, the latter could not hide her impression. The walls of the two rooms were painted off-white, the ceiling was painted sky-blue, and the furniture and the carpet were a combination of light brown and ivory. The bed cover was light blue with white pillowcases to match. The window blinds and curtains completed the beautiful combination of the choice of furnishing of the rooms. The toilet was all white. The color scheme and the brightness of the rooms blended to uplift the soul of anybody in it.

Blessing told Owen how wonderful the combination of colors in the rooms was and how everything fitted in, together. It reminded her of her own house, how everything was immaculately clean and in its right place. She wondered how Owen could have imagined that. It could have been a coincidence or a meeting of minds, she thought. Owen informed his guest that they would go out for dinner later, told her how to contact him or the house-keeper for anything she needed, and left the room.

Blessing felt some excitement since her arrival. This was out of tune with her usual cool, calculated perception of situations. Something was gradually stirring up on the inside, and she could not say what it was or what caused it. She felt at home in the guest room, and she was equally very pleased to see Owen again. After the chance meeting in the bank, she had been thinking about Owen, which to her, was odd and out of character. She was thinking of what to tell Owen when she heard a knock on the door. It was 6:30 PM, and she knew that it was Owen coming to take her out for dinner. She was dressed and ready.

When the door opened, there was another surprise; the two of them dressed formally in suits of similar color. Blessing wore a brown skirt, light yellow blouse, and brown coat while Owen appeared in a brown suit over a white shirt and a red tie. Both of them wore brown shoes. They looked at each other. *Was that a coincidence or meeting of minds?* They seemed to think. Blessing read more into the matching dress; she recalled the circumstance of their first meeting in Lagos, then the choice of colors in the guest room she occupied. Owen complimented her in her dressing and took her hand to lead her down to the wait-ing car.

The Metropolitan Hotel was a short drive from Owen's house. It was a leading rendezvous for the elite in the city, and that was to where Owen and Blessing headed. The hotel was one of few top places to go for good food and fine drinks in the city, a choice place for the elite.

Blessing felt at ease with Owen. It was the first time they would sit down together and talk. Owen chose the drinks and asked Blessing to choose the food. It was as if they had known each other for years; they talked about many things, including personal things. As the drinks and food arrived, they were pleased with each other's choice.

Owen was very much impressed; Blessing was knowledgeable in very many subjects. As a senior bank officer in a management position, she was used to attending social events. She acted naturally and comfortably in Owen's company. And for the first time in many years since Oma died, Owen found comfort in a woman's company. He had denied himself that luxury of socializing with women in all those years.

By 9:30 PM, they were back to the house. They sat down again to talk over some drinks before Owen took her to her room and bid her a good night. She went to bed satisfied and very happy about the events of the day. For the first time in her life, she felt something differently. She tried to recall the feeling she had after seeing Owen in Lagos about a month earlier. That feeling was spontaneous, and the more she tried to suppress it, the stronger it became, that feeling which urged her to speak to Owen. She believed it was a cosmic arrangement for her to meet Owen. She, however, cautioned herself not to come to a hasty conclusion. After all, she had one week to stay with Owen.

CHAPTER ELEVEN
TURN OF EVENTS

The driver from the bank picked up Ms. Blessing Bassey and drove her to the bank to start her duty. Her temporary duty would last one week and the driver would remain with her for the duration. She met the branch manager of the bank, briefed him, and outlined how she intended to proceed with her assignment. Ms Bassey was always very precise and disciplined when it came to her work, always thoughtful and anticipatory, and left nothing to chance.

Surprisingly, she did not make any demands on the manager, which was most unusual with a visiting officer. She accepted a courtesy dinner to be hosted by the bank that evening. Following usual practice, she could invite a non-bank staff as her guest for the dinner. She immediately called Owen to request if he would be able to attend. The answer was spontaneous: he would go with her.

The dinner that evening went on well; it was what it was meant to be—a welcome dinner in honor of a senior officer from the bank headquarters. It was a policy the bank officers loved because it afforded them the opportunity to feel the pulse of headquarters about the branch.

The officers discussed freely; Ms. Bassey was articulate and uncompromising and satisfied their expectations. When it was over, they all felt happy that she was the one who was sent. They were also very happy to see her company. Dr. Owen was the most prominent customer the bank had in the city and one of the most respectable citizens in the state.

For the one week Blessing spent in Calabar, she would leave the house at 8:00 in the morning and work throughout in the bank until 5:00 in the evening. At the same time, she told Owen that she would be preparing dinner in the house and ruled out going to the restaurant to eat. How she did it, Owen did not understand. Dinner was always ready at 8:00. She never asked Owen for money. She provided everything she needed in the house. Owen experienced a new kind of life for the duration of Blessing's stay in the house.

Blessing was meticulous in her management. Each morning before she left for work, she would instruct the housekeeper on what to do. She was always specific in the instructions. If there was anything to be purchased for dinner, she would provide the funds. By the time she arrived home from work, everything she needed for dinner was ready. And when she went into the kitchen, it was cooking time. The product was always fantastic dish for dinner. The practice was so standard and routine that it regulated Owen's evening arrangement for one week.

Owen discovered that he and Blessing had very many things in common. He was a very orderly man, and so was Blessing. There was compatibility in the choice of dress, choice of food, manner of speech, and even the way each of them walked. They both worked hard and thrived for perfection. During the little shopping she made before going back to Lagos, Blessing always went for the best, and Owen did not fail to notice that. They had talked enough to conclude that they could live happily under one roof, but neither of them mentioned anything close to that. One thing was sure: they were two friends just waiting to meet, and destiny brought them together. Destiny, indeed. Owen believed in destiny.

There was one thing Owen saw that was missing in Blessing's life. She was a lonely woman. For all the time they were talking, she never mentioned anything about her family or relations or friends. Owen avoided asking her specifically about that but wondered how such a beautiful, well educated, well-groomed, and apparently well-to-do young lady could stay without friends. Was there anything she wanted to hide? Definitely, that was not the case.

Blessing finished her assignment in the bank in Calabar and returned to Lagos. She returned to Lagos a changed woman. She believed that she had found what she had been waiting for all her life, a man she could love and live with. But did she make a mistake not to ask him for something she only assumed he would give her? But that was not her nature; she always believed that she could get anything she needed without overtly asking for it.

Blessing never talked about her family. According to her, she had no father, not even a step-father. She was not yet five when her mother told her that her father was killed in the civil war, which started about six months after she was born. Blessing grew up in her grandmother's one bedroom house where her mother also lived. Things were difficult with them, and the grandmother made a lot of sacrifices to provide for her minimal needs as a child. Life became much tougher for her when the grandmother died by the time she was six.

Since Blessing was four years old, her mother had no gainful employment and no means of providing for her. She used to work in the big cement factory in town but was laid off among many other workers when the factory could no longer break even. There were no known relations to help the mother, as was the culture among the people. Melody, Blessing's mother, started the business of sex for money to fend for herself and her child. First, they were two or three men who visited her from time to time, but later, it became a regular flow of men of all characters coming in and out, day and night. It soon became talk of the town.

For little Blessing, the men were too many for her to notice any of them as the father figure she needed in her life, and she started to resent their presence in the house. Her resentment created some problems for the mother in her business. Little Blessing had to be sent to the village school immediately when she reached age five, one year below the normal age. She was able to stay away from home most of the day, and that allowed her mother to do her business uninterrupted. As a concession, as it were, the mother regulated the number of visitors in the night.

Blessing was a gifted child. In spite of the handicap in her upbringing, she did extremely well in school. Her teachers were astonished in the number of things she knew. At seven, she could solve mathematical problems for 11-year-old students. She could write and discuss issues when her classmates were still struggling with the construction of their first sentence.

Blessing was seven years old when one day she refused to go home after school. She said that she did not want to live with her mother any more. Because she could not be forced to go home, the school headmaster accepted the responsibility to keep her for a few days until a permanent home could be found for her. An expatriate Methodist Reverend Minister offered to keep Blessing in his family. She was taken away from the village, and the crisis averted. Blessing never returned to the village since then.

In retrospect, one could see why Blessing had no known family relations. Rev. Wilcox was the only man she knew as a "father." She revolted against the kind of life her mother lived and rejected her. She never turned back to look for the mother again. She did all her education outside where she was born; she made new friends and relations and had no need to search for relations other than those she knew. It was not long after Blessing was taken in by Rev. Wilcox that the latter was posted to a new station in Umuahia. He took Blessing with him.

Meanwhile, Melody was forced to leave the village. She set up shop in the city where she continued to ply her trade without any molestation. Years later, according to information which filtered into the village, she followed one of her lovers to Equatorial Guinea, the Island of Fernando Po, as it was known locally, a tiny country, south of Nigeria, across the Gulf of Guinea.

After her elementary school education where Blessing always remained on top of her class, she gained admission into Ovim Girls School, Ovim. Ovim Girls school was one of the leading mission institutions in Eastern Nigeria by then. She was only 11. For five years, she continued to dominate and maintain a first position in all her classes. She was still under the guardianship of Reverend Minister Wilcox, who was now stationed in Umuahiah, a town not too far away from Ovim.

Blessing was unstoppable. She entered the University of Ibadan in Western Nigeria before she celebrated her eighteenth birthday. All along, she had been studying on government scholarship, and now she was a federal government scholar, which meant that the financial provision that followed the award was sufficient to meet all her needs. She also received other internal awards based on her exceptional academic performance. Blessing went through the university financially self-sufficient, and for the first time, she was able to manage herself. At 21, Blessing graduated First Class in Economics. Two years later, she received her Master's degree with specialization in Finance and Banking.

Blessing was as beautiful as she was brilliant, but she remained an enigma when it came to relations with men. Her relationship with her male classmates, or other men for that matter, was not beyond a normal friendly relationship. Men were falling head-over-heels seeking her love.

She had a way of warding them off without being offensive. She never showed any sexual interest in men; she was not a lesbian either. There was something deep rooted on the inside that she never understood, and for her, it never mattered. In spite of what men saw as abnormal in her, Blessing led a very happy and normal life. She associated freely with both men and women.

Apart from the excellent academic performance in school and in the university, Blessing also excelled in sports and other extracurricular activities. She won trophies in individual field events; she was the president of her high school debate club, she was the chairperson of her hall of residence in the university, The Queen's Hall. She was a leader her peers always looked up to, and she never disappointed them.

Blessing was recruited by the First Bank before she finished her Master's program. The First Bank was at that time a leading Nigerian bank. Blessing assumed duty in the bank immediately she dropped her pen. She was appointed a senior banking officer from where she started her career. At the time Owen met her in the bank in Lagos, she had risen to the rank of a senior manager in charge of operations.

Back in Lagos, Blessing settled into her work, but she was a different woman. Life seemed to assume a different meaning for her after the one-week official trip to Calabar that afforded her the opportunity to meet Owen again. She was always on the telephone with Owen every morning before she started work and the last thing before she went to bed. They remained in constant communication.

On few occasions, usually pubic holidays or weekends, Blessing visited Owen at his invitation. The bond between the two was becoming stronger by the day.

After five months of regular contact, Owen felt that he had understood Blessing well enough to propose to her. Her feeling for Owen was real; Owen's wealth and celebrity standing was beside the point. Besides her physical beauty, Blessing was a very confident and respectable woman. From the quality of her wardrobe, and everything about her, she was well-to-do and independent. But women are unpredictable creatures when it comes to the issues of the heart and the world of materialism. Owen had come to see Blessing differently. So, he travelled to Lagos on this special weekend to propose to her. Blessing had been expecting it. They celebrated it at a dinner that night. There were no witnesses when Owen slipped in the engagement ring on her finger. Owen returned to Calabar the following afternoon.

There were no relations to be consulted, so two of them decided on a date for the wedding. They allowed just enough time for preparations to be made. It promised to be an elaborate wedding. The only two people Owen was obligated to inform were his children, Ben and Bassey. Ben was now 24 and was just starting his Ph.D. program in aeronautic engineering, while Bassey was in a medical school also in Harvard. Ben and Bassey would attend the wedding of their father and Blessing.

For Owen and Blessing, life continued to be normal. Their relationship was on a different level now. Their communication was between a wife and a husband who were waiting for the bells to toll. Blessing was making more frequent visits to Calabar to consult with people who were engaged in the wedding arrangement. She also had to discuss with Owen about the wedding gown, which was coming from Lagos.

Owen got a surprise call one day, one month after his engagement. Blessing was transferred to Calabar as the branch manager of the First Bank there. This was good news for both Owen and Blessing; they would now be residing in the same city. As a top management officer, Blessing knew that there was an ongoing process to move top management staff around, but she had no clue that it would affect her. It was, however, not a complete surprise because she had spent 12 of her 15 years in the bank in Lagos area alone. What was a pleasant surprise was that she was sent to Calabar.

Blessing arrived in Calabar to resume duty and moved into her official residence. Her movement to Calabar fitted very well into her wedding plans. She was now closer to Owen, and they could easily work together. It was easier for her to combine her heavy responsibility in the bank and getting things together for her up-coming wedding.

CHAPTER TWELVE
THE WEDDING

The sensational wedding card read Benjamin Bassey Weds Blessing Bassey, date Saturday August, 21, 2005. The omission of Owen was deliberate. In the locality, two events usually pull large crowds—weddings and funerals. This one was not just a wedding; it was Benjamin Owen's wedding. The bride was also a woman of substance in the society. A wealthy businessman, a philanthropist, and a social crusader and the bank manager were getting married.

Preparation for the wedding went into full gear as soon as Blessing arrived in Calabar. Experts and professionals in the business were consulted and engaged. Every detail was taken care of, and rehearsals were conducted. The wedding gown came from Lagos. The groom suit came from the United States. The decoration for the maidens and the flower girls came from China. The wedding was a blending of the western society wedding and the rich Efik cultural wedding.

Their wedding day is usually a special day in the life of the couple. This was a special day in Blessing's life. As was expected, thousands descended on the town. It was a roll call of WHO'S WHO in the state and beyond. Bank officials were in attendance to witness the wedding ceremony of one of their own. Members of the community trooped out in their numbers to be counted. It was an opportunity for the many benefitiaries of Owen's humanitarian activities to show their solidarity with him.

The town stood still. All routes led to the town cathedral where the wedding was conducted. The town folks illuminated the cathedral in their Sunday best. The VIPs competed in their fancy tailored suits and traditional attire. The cathedral was filled to capacity. The overflow watched the ceremony on a big television screen mounted outside the cathedral.

The atmosphere was serene as the nuptial train moved into the cathedral. Owen accompanied by his bestman Ben first went in. The son of Rev. Minister Wilcox escorted the bride and stood in for the father Blessing never knew. Later, he would give her out for marriage according to tradition. The bride appeared in a white sartin wedding gown with blue stones. Her head was decorated with multi-colored traditional beads. She used a very light make-up from a traditional camwood mixture.

The bridesmaids almost stole the show in their blown blue dress above the knee and the legs covered in beads. The flower girls were dubbed little angels. Their uniform of multi-colored fabric could make them be mistaken for the Chinese muppet show. They were admirable. The bell boys came in with their own uniqueness to add colour to the scenery. Owen and Blessing were joined in a solemn matrimonial ceremony watched by thousands of friends and well wishers. They were declared husband and wife.

From the cathedral, guests converged at the reception venue. It was held in an open space to accumudate the thousands who turned up. The reception program was elaborate and strictly followed. Prayers were offered. Speeches were made. Others sang and danced in celebration. And soon it was time for the new couple to perform their first dance. They danced to the melody of the music to the admiration of the guests. By tradition, this was the time for quests to show appreciation for the beautiful dance performed by the couple. That meant showering them with money and joining them in dancing. Everybody was on their feet as the quests showed that they came prepared to celebrate with the couple.

There was enough food and drink for everybody. The reception continued late into the evening before it finally ended. This was the wedding of the century.

Among the wedding guests was one person Owen specially invited with all expences paid. He was Captain Buhari, by now, a retired Colonel. Over the years, Owen did not forget Buhari, the first officer he met when he walked into the hands of the federal troops. He still remembered that moment he thanked Captain Buhari and told him that they would meet again.

Two days after the historic wedding, the couple flew out of the country on their honeymoon. There was something peculiar, or maybe unique, in the honeymoon. The couple did not know where they were going to spend the honeymoon until a day before their departure. The arrangement was contracted to the professionals who handled the entire wedding arrangement. It was part of the contract. They used their professionalism, imagination, and experience to create and work out every detail for the honeymoon. The couple had fully paid for it without knowing anything about it.

The choice of the places was as surprising as it was meant to be. Quite far off from what they were thinking, the couple was billed to go to India, Nepal, and Bhutan in Asia. These were not places they had imagined they would go to spend their honeymoon. That was the surprise and the "fun." India could be in the realm of possibility, but certainly not Nepal and Bhutan, which were the main focus of the trip. The couple would spend two nights in India, three nights each in Nepal and Bhutan at the foot of the Himalayas.

Honeymoon is a time to relax after the hectic period and anxiety of the wedding. Apart from relaxation, the places chosen for them would teach them a little something. Geographically, culturally, and socio-economically, Bhutan and Nepal presented them with something uncommon.

Bhutan is described as the "land of festivals," where the national development is measured in the happiness of the people. Other countries talk about "Gross National Product" (GNP). In Bhutan, it is "Gross National Happiness" (GNH). The people live one day at a time in a seemingly life of contentment. There appears to be no animosity among the people. Everyday life seems to be without fear or anxiety. The infrastructure is not the best in the world, but everybody moves around happily making a living. Religion appears to influence their lives.

In Nepal, shadowed by the great Himalayas, people

struggle and live with the hope that there is always a to-morrow. Kathmandu, the capital, is "home of the divine," "residence of the living god," and the "garden of dream." When the couple arrived at the Monkey temple, they concluded that Nepal was a land of wonders.

In India, the couple went straight fron New Delhi to Agra to see the famed Taj Mahal, an inspirational, hypnotizing white marble palace, an emblem of love. They enjoyed their ride on elephants and the wonderful sight of road sharing by animals, human beings, and everything that moves on wheels. Every inch of India represented something unique to the couple. They saw the old and the new blended together in a seemingly pepertual competition.

It was a wonderful time for Mr. and Mrs. Owen. Everywhere in the three countries they went was a tourist sight. It was a well-planned trip, from the food they ate, their accommodations, and the things they saw, to the people they met and the first-hand experiences they had in a land so different from what they had known. They were full of admiration for the professionalism, expertise, and imagination of the agents who organized it for them. The couple returned after 10 days of bliss and life in wonderland.

The couple settled into their new life of husband and wife. Blessing continued to serve in the bank as the manager while Owen focused fully on his flourishing business and service to society. By now, Blessing has moved from her official bank quarters into her matrimonial home. They were comfortable and happy.

It was barely 11 months when the couple had their first child. He was named CocoBassey. His birth called for an ocassion of celebration. It was time for Mrs. Owen to leave the bank after many years of meritorious service. The birth of her son provided a good opportunity to do so. She tendered her resignation accordingly as soon as she completed her maternity leave.

Mrs. Owen started a new kind of life. It was difficult at first to stay all day at home. She started to get used to it and enjoyed the privilage of choosing what to do and when to do it.

It was not long when the Owens got a second child. It was three years after the wedding. The girl was named Joy. Joy's birth was celebrated in a grand style. With the help of a nanny, the burden of taking care of the children was greatly reduced.

Life continued to be a bed of roses for the Owens. Blessing was now taking active part in the running of the growing family business. She took charge of the Finance Houses, brought in innovations and expanded it to cover areas which were not covered before. The various social and economic development activities in the community sponsored by Owen & Associates Architectual Design were formalized and linked to a foundation to ensure their continuity.

The "Bless Owen Foundation" was incorporated and run as a non-governmental organization (NGO), with Mrs. Blessing Owen as the Chief Executive Officer (CEO). Life for Mrs. Owen was busier than ever. She had the organization to run, a family with two children to look after, and increasing social events to organize or attend. She took part in regular life Television programs on social issues. She was fully out-stretched.

CHAPTER THIRTEEN

THE RETURN OF MELODY

Sometime in 2009, unknown to Mrs. Owen, her mother, Melody Bassey came back from Equatorial Guinea where she had spent the last 35 years. She was 64 and only very few people in the village remembered her. She could not find an accommodation in the village, so she drifted back to the city where she shared a rented apartment with an old friend.

Melody came back a changed woman, or maybe she was too old to engage in her former trade. She opened a small retail shop in the neighborhood where she lived. She also ran a retail telephone business beside the shop. The retail telephone shop, with four cellular telephones became real money-spinning business for Melody. People were moving in and out, making telephone calls and patronizing the retail shop. Melody's place soon became a center for gossip and rumour peddling.

Melody's return had no effect on Blessing. As a matter of fact, the mother had long ceased to be a factor in her life; for all the years, Blessing never knew where she was or never cared or even remembered that she had a mother.

Likewise, if Melody ever thought of her daughter, she shared no such thoughts with anybody.

One day, as she was watching the television, Melody saw a woman called Mrs. Owen featuring in a public enlightenment program and recognized her as her daughter, Blessing.

Before that moment, Melody did not remember anything about the daughter who ran away from her more than 35 years ago. She did not make any attempt to find out where the daughter was when she came back, but seeing her daughter on the television screen after so many years evoked some maternal emotions she was not able to control. That feeling came naturally and set in motion the anxiety to see the daughter.

She started asking questions about Mrs. Owen. The Owens were a household name in the city. Besides, this was a place where one could readily find people who volunteered information, so it did not really take long before Melody knew all she needed to know about the daughter and her husband. She also located where they lived. But she was afraid to go to the house and ask for Blessing, fearing that having abandoned her for so long, she would not recognize her as the mother. She preferred to approach the house unnoticed, but unfortunately for her, the location of the house made such an adventure difficult, if not impossible.

It was late in the evening when Melody made her third attempt to look into the house. She chose a very auspicious time; the rooms on the ground floor of the house were brightly lid, but it was not dark enough to switch on the lights outside. It was easier for the person standing outside to see the house than vice-versa. From an upper floor room, Owen saw a figure standing at the kitchen window and went down to have a closer look. She was an elderly woman, unarmed, but still, he had to approach the figure cautiously.

Owen moved close enough to recognize her as Melody, although he had not met her for more than 30 years. Their eyes met. She was still gazing into the kitchen as Owen moved closer to question her presence there. Owen did not call her by name but gestured to her to go nearer. Instead, Melody sprang back like a teenage girl and started talking.

"Don't touch me," she shouted, as she tried to flee the scene, "you have committed an abomination. That is my child. Where did you find her?" she continued as she pointed to the kitchen. "They told me about you, so it is true. I cannot live to see this. She is your daughter. You are her father. This is an abomination."

Owen was dumfounded. He had heard enough from Melody, and he heard her very well. But he needed to talk to her. After the outburst, she fled the scene, and Owen thought he could pursue and catch up with her but changed his mind. Owen knew that he was not dreaming; he heard her clearly. He went back into the house, sat down alone, and started to think of those words, "That is my child, she is your daughter".

Owen decided to look for Melody wherever she may be. It was getting dark, so that search would start in the morning. He needed to hear the full story from her. Owen heard Melody very clearly. She was old but not crazy. Was it the ranting of a jealous old woman?

Owen pulled himself together as he went through the memory of relationship with Melody. He promised to look for Melody the following day. That was not to be. That next day, some fishermen sighted a floating body off Henshaw town beach and called the police. The lifeless body of a woman was pulled out of the water. The body was that of Melody. It was not identified until two days later. Meanwhile, Owen had been quietly trying to find her until he stumbled on the news of an elderly woman who got drowned. Melody had told Owen that she could not live to see the union. Owen confirmed that the dead woman was Melody.

Melody was laid to rest without any fanfare, paid for by one of Owen's charity organizations since she had no means or relations to pay for her burial. She was not identified with Owen in any way, neither was she traced to Blessing. Luckily, the drama between her and Owen a day before her death was not witnessed by any person, and events moved so fast that Owen had no time to tell anybody about it.

Melody lived an inglorious life and died an abominable death. If there was any truth in what she said, it meant that she lied to a man who would have probably married her and also lied to her child before she was old enogh to understand.

O O O

Those words continued to ring in his ears: "I cannot live to see this, she is your daughter, it is an abomination..."

Owen tried to dismiss them as mere rantings of a desperate jealous old woman who had wasted her life pursuing worthless ends and had decided to take her own life in frustration. Melody was not known for her honesty or integrity, but her waywardness did not make her crazy. What would she have lost if she had gone to take her life without telling Owen that his wife was his daughter?

Owen was emotionally disturbed and physically shaken. As much as he tried to conceal his feelings, Blessing knew he was not fine, but he insisted that all was fine. He tried to keep out of the wife's way in the pretense that he was very busy. Owen thought he could surpress the thoughts permanently, but the more he tried, the more they came up violently. After a disturbing one week since the encounter with Melody, Owen decided to hold the bull by the horn and put the issue to rest.

First, Owen established a timeline since the time he first met Melody about 42 years earlier. Secondly, he would investigate the circumstances surrounding Blessing, beginning from the time of her birth through her early childhood to the time Owen met her in Lagos. The second sprung of investigation was to establish that the Blessing Owen met in Lagos was the same Blessing who was Melody's child in order to confirm Melody' story.

Owen recalled that he spent his long vacation from the university in the summer of 1966 in Calabar. He took a vacation job in the ministry of Town Planning. It was while on vacation that he met Melody. Melody was a dazzling, beautiful, hair dresser. She was about 21 years old. Melody and Owen, who was then called Bassey, fell in love with each other. This was about the beginning of July 1966. The two spent most of the time together and had all the fun as first-time lovers. Throughout the summer months, the two lovers lived in a world of their own. Then came October when Bassey had to return to the university.

By end of September, Melody realized that she was pregnant, by which time Owen was already back in school. Communication between them was sporadic. It was not until end of the year Owen learned that Melody was pregnant. Melody's child was born in March 1967. Owen did not deny the paternity of the child. He saw the mother and child once before the war broke out.

The next time Owen met Melody, she was not with the child. Melody told him that the child had died. Owen recalled that although he was skeptical about the information, he had no real reason not to believe her. Owen made his calculations and came to a conclusion. Assuming that Melody had lied to Owen about the death of the child and that the child lived to be an adult, she would be the same age as Blessing. Therefore, if that child was alive, contrary to what the mother said, she could be Blessing.

Owen did not want to rush to a definitive conclusion because he believed other facts could prove him wrong. So, he started the investigation that would take him out to other places and people.

Owen had to find a convenient excuse to travel to the village where Blessing was born. He drove himself to the village, which was not far from the town. Owen's strategy was to speak to random people of about 60 years of age who were likely to remember Melody. It was not as difficult as Owen thought. Within one hour of his arrival in the village, he accosted two men separately who collaborated their story.

Each of them told Owen that they remembered Blessing as the small girl who revolted against her mother's notorious living and ran away from her. They confirmed that a white man took Blessing away and that they never saw her or the mother again in the village. Owen heard more than enough to comfirm the story's authenticity, thanks to a community where everybody knew everybody else and people were ready and prepared to volunteer information, even to perfect strangers.

The white man referred to by the villagers was Reverend Minister Wilcox, who had since passed on in England. The son who stood in for Blessing's father during the wedding was easy to reach. He was eager and happy to talk about Blessing. He extolled her brilliance and tenacity, and that she was a woman guided by God. He charted her educational performance in high school and in the university. He did not fail to commend Blessing's high moral standard.

There was nothing more Owen needed to confirm that the small girl who revolted against the mother and taken away from the village was the Blessing he met in a bank in Lagos.

Blessing never talked about her family, because, according to her, she had none. Her father, according to the mother, was killed in the civil war before she had the opportunity to know him. The mother she knew abandoned her to pursue her passion. The grandmother she knew died at the time she needed her most as a child. She grew up with a perfect stranger, although a benevolent man, he did not make himself acceptable, even as a step-father.

She loved Rev. Wilcox and would have accepted him as a father if he wanted it. Reverent Wilcox left Nigeria and handed Blessing to another care taker instead of taking her to England as a father would do. Blessing grew up with no relations or any person she could deem as a family member.

Indeed, Melody had told her little girl that her father was killed in the civil war, which ended by the time she was three years old. She had also told Owen that the little girl he saw once had died. It was unfathomable what her intention was. Whatever her reason, her action was unforgivable.

Beyond the conclusion Owen reached in his investigation and encouraged by it, he sat back to rethink of the sequence of events since he met Blessing in Lagos. First, it was the electrifying effect on Owen when he saw Blessing. Owen saw his picture before him—Blessing resembled Owen in many ways. She was almost as tall as Owen. There were some common mannerisms in them. The same names, Owen waived as common in their ethnic community. For the first time in more than five years, Owen felt drawn to a woman. Blessing was always on his mind after the first meeting.

What was coincidental in all these? Owen asked himself. Owen recalled many other things, like the choice of colours, dress, and food, which he usually attributed to the meeting of the minds. He sat there, buried in his thoughts. He realized that there had been too many coincidences, too many meetings of the minds, to be ignored. The two had been attracted to each other like magnets. There had been that overwhelming evidence that the little girl Blessing, who revolted against the mother and left the village, grew up to be the Blessing Owen met in Lagos on that fateful day.

Owen looked again into the chain of events in his life. He did not follow his instincts when he left Norfolk and relocated in Oklahoma, and stayed longer there than he had planned. He remembered the cool night in May 1999 that he sat and passed out on the debris of his house with his wife and children buried under. Were these and other happenings part of the scheme to lead him home to unite with his lost daughter? Why did he have to lose his loving wife and children in order to discover his daughter? Were their lives worth nothing? Was his life spared so that he could continue the adventure? Was there no other way for him to have discovered his daughter without marrying her? Why did Melody appear on the scene to spill the beans? Owen did not have any answer to all these intrigueing questions. He knew he had an issue to contend with.

Owen could no longer pretend that Melody was wrong. He had accepted the paternity of the child 43 years ago, and now that child was his wife. Fortunately, he remained the only person who knew this fact. Melody died with the knowledge. Owen could not turn back the hands of the clock. The problem for him was how to relate the fact to Blessing, or not to let her know at all.

After a long thought, Owen came to the conclusion that Blessing had the right to know but was doubtful how she would receive it. For that reason, he decided not to tell Blessing. For Owen, it was remarkable the way he handled it. He showed no sign that something out of place had happened. He still loved and adored Blessing, whether as a wife or as a daughter. Nothing changed in the relationship. They continued their life as husband and wife. If there was to be any crisis, it would be with Owen; but he showed no signs.

Owen felt that he was not honest and fair to Blessing to keep the discovery back from her. But at the same time, the need to protect her from any emotional breakdown or permanent damage to their relationship overpowered the urge to let her know. Then finally, after pushing the idea up and down, Owen accepted the need for Blessing to know because it was also about her. But it would be later, and that time would be after his demise. He did not have the advantage of being advised by anyone, so whatever decision he came to was the dictate of his mind and the circumstance.

He therefor planned to address a letter to Blessing, in which he would tell her the story in full. The letter would be for her eyes only and kept in a sealed container that would be opened only when Owen passed on. After agreeing with himself, Owen got to work on the letter.

It read:

My dear Blessing,

I loved you from the day we set our eyes on each other. I never turned back since then. You were everything and all I needed in life until it was my time to depart.

There is only one thing I hid from you, for which I am apologizing. Many years ago, a woman got drowned off Henshaw beach. It was actually a suicide. That woman was Melody, your mother.

She was at our house the day before she died and saw you through the kitchen window. I saw her, recognized her, and went to talk to her. She said many things and ran away. Things which I tried very hard and kept away from you. I apologize again for that. I believed then that it was in our best interest that you did not know.

She said things like, "She is my daughter; you are her father," referring to you and me. Before she finally ran into the dark street, she said that she would not live to see what was an abomination, meaning our marriage. Then she went to take her life.

The thing is, that I met Melody the year before you were born. We fell in love, and it appeared that you were the product of our relationship. Don't forget that it is only the woman who knows the father of her own child. You were born few months before the civil war started in 1967. I fought in that war as an officer. Melody lied to me that you were dead. From my investigation, she also lied to you that I was killed during the war. I don't want to make a guess or to blame Melody why she lied to two of us; judgement belongs to God.

We met in an unusual circumstance and stuck to each other since then. You bear my name, which I took as a coincidence when we first met. I loved and adored you, whether as a daughter or as a wife. Did it really matter who we were.? We did not know it. We did not need to blame ourselves. I did not blame or condemn us. The invisible hands which brought us together know better than us mere mortals.

You have the right to know our true relationship. Forgive me for witholding it from you for so long. It was difficult for me to deal with it. Do not be disturbed. Continue to live your life. You are the only person alive who know this story. It is true that you are my daughter, my wife, and my true love. Nature has conived to play us the trick. I was not aware of anything we could have done differently. Was this our destiny?

You are at liberty to tell our children, if you consider it right for them to know. But it may be advisable to let it stop with us, and free the children from any shadow over their lives.

God bless you. We shall meet again in another incarnation.

Ben

It took days for Owen to finish the letter. He sat back and questioned himself again of the necessity of writing the letter he knew would cause the wife great emotional upset. His belief that there was a reason for everything that happened in his life always overrode his reasoning. Destiny was a good explanation for inexplicable actions or events in his life. It sometimes justified the laissez-faire attitude to life events.

Life was not normal anymore with Owen, whatever he thought. The knowledge that his daughter was his wife constantly haunted him. He knew that was not normal in modern civilized cultural arrangements. He accepted it as part of his destiny, but his inner mind's revolt was still troubling him since the time, he knew the truth. For Blessing, life was still normal, and Owen made sure he did not let down his guard. He was successful in playing the game for many years that he almost forgot the truth.

O   O   O

Owen had to visit the United States again to see his doctor. The cancer that was diagnosed some years ago and treated came back again. This time, it was spreading to the brain. The diagnosis was not good. In the opinion of the doctor, Owen had few months to live. This was, however, not disclosed to the patient, so the treatment continued.

There was very little improvement in his health in all the period he spent in the hospital. Owen perceived that the end was near after weeks of agony.

As he lay listless on the bed, he wondered what was going to happen to him. He knew that the coronavirus pandemic was spreading rapidly and tried to think as much as his strength could carry him. He knew that his wife and children were still there. They all knew that the end was near and that it was a matter of moments.

Owen opened his eyes one more time; his wife held his hand. That seemed to have been enough goodbye. He closed his eyes again, and with it went his last breath. There, Benjamin Owen passed on peacefully. His wife and his two elder children, Ben and Bassey, were at his bedside when he gave up. He was 72 years old.

Owen died in the United States in April 2020. This was the time the coronavirus pandemic caused panic everywhere, and there were traffic restrictions. Owen's body could not be flown back to the place he called home for burial. Owen was interned in a place he lived as a visitor and once referred to as a very good host. What an irony!

Benjamin Bassey Owen was laid to rest like a pauper. There were no celebrations, no roll call of very important people at the funeral, no crowd of the people whose lives he touched, no mourners. There was no rostrum on which to read his impressive biography. Owen started life with a clear focus on what he wanted to get out of it. In the process, he encountered obstacles, but none were able to hold him back. He reached the pinnacle of life and reached out to lift others up, which is considered the greatest good. He went down marrying his own daughter and passed on at a time and in a place, he could not be celebrated. Was that his destiny? Is this destiny?

Post Script

After Owen's interment in the United States, Blessing spent another six months in the country. The coronavirus pandemic was still raging on like wild fire everywhere, and to curb its spread, many countries, incluing the United States and Nigeria, imposed travel restrictions in and out of their territories. Therefore, Blessing was unable to leave the United States for home. She finally returned to Nigeria alone in November 2020.

Her priority attention at home was focused on the children she did not see for one year; she spent most of the time with them as if to make up for their one-year separation. She almost forgot the sealed envelope Benjamin left for her "for her eyes only." When she remembered it, she needed time alone to read it and decided to do it in the dead of the night when the children were in bed.

She did not know what to expect. With her grief continuing to torture her, she did not imagine that something more tormenting was in wait for her. All alone at night, she opened the envelope and started to read the letter. Blessing was a strong woman, but halfway through the letter, she passed out. There was nobody to help her. She lay helpless for about two hours before she was able to regain her consciousness, then she gathered her strength and calmly read through the piece. She did not need a second reading to understand it. She resolved that Melody was a mother who was absent in her entire life and, when she resurfaced, decided to kill her joy.

Benjamin was the only man she loved in her life. She got married to him. Whether or not he was her father was inconsequential.

"He might have been my father; he was my lover; he was my husband; he was the father of my children; he was my all," she told herself.

Blessing was strong, courageous, and resolute. She decided to be the only other person to know about the letter and the only living person to know the truth about the relationship between Benjamin and herself. That morning, Blessing burned the letter and buried the memory of it with the ashes.